THE FILE ON ANGELYN STARK

THE FILE

ON

ANGELYN STARK

a novel by

CATHERINE ATKINS

EMBER

Text copyright © 2011 by Catherine Atkins
Cover art copyright © 2011 by Getty Images

All rights reserved. Published in the United States by Ember, an imprint of Random House Children's Books, a division of Random House, Inc., New York. Originally published in hardcover in the United States by Alfred A. Knopf, an imprint of Random House Children's Books, New York, in 2011.

Ember and the E colophon are registered trademarks of Random House, Inc.

Visit us on the Web! randomhouse.com/teens

Educators and librarians, for a variety of teaching tools,
visit us at randomhouse.com/teachers

The Library of Congress has cataloged the hardcover edition of this work as follows:
Atkins, Catherine.
The file on Angelyn Stark / Catherine Atkins. — 1st ed.
            p. cm.
Summary: Fifteen-year-old Angelyn Stark, a troubled high school student, is trying to get along while keeping a terrible secret about her past, but when one of her teachers tries to offer her encouragement and support, she does not know how to react.
ISBN 978-0-375-86906-8 (trade) — ISBN 978-0-375-96906-5 (lib. bdg.) —
ISBN 978-0-375-89989-8 (ebook)
[1. Secrets—Fiction. 2. Family problems—Fiction. 3. Sexual abuse—Fiction.
4. Teacher-student relationships—Fiction. 5. High schools—Fiction.
6. Schools—Fiction.] I. Title.
PZ7.A862Fi 2011
[Fic]—dc23
2011016681

ISBN 978-0-375-87313-3 (pbk.)

Printed in the United States of America

10 9 8 7 6 5 4 3 2 1

First Ember Edition 2012

Random House Children's Books supports the First Amendment and celebrates the right to read.

To Michele and Ginger

With thanks to the real Miss Bass, Jim Atkins, Sarah Carrillo,
Cindy Dodge, and everyone who read for me,
especially Amanda Jenkins.

CHAPTER ONE

Angelyn, Fifteen

New girl walks through the three of us smoking in the bathroom. Jacey and me on the sinks, our long legs dangling. Charity, opposite, leaning against a partition.

"She must think she's hot," Charity says as the girl disappears into a stall.

I try and think if I've seen her before. One thing's for sure.

New girl doesn't know about us.

You don't use *this* bathroom without asking first. Not during morning break.

Ten-thirty to ten-forty, Monday through Friday, the second-floor Vocational Building girls' room belongs to us. Everybody knows it.

We snicker when we hear the girl peeing. As if we've never done *that*. Charity moves to the stall and thumps a fist against the door. Once. Twice. The flow stops. And starts. Jacey and I exchange a grin.

"Thinks she's so cool," Jacey says when the girl comes out. She's scared. Dark eyes taking us in. Ballerina body. Charity's in her face, twice her size.

I push off from the sink. Jacey does too. I flick my cigarette to the drain. Jacey drops hers on the floor. I'm warm watching the girl squirm, warm in my stomach like I've just had cocoa. Curious too. Excited. I'm not bored.

We take Charity's back, a triangle of tough.

"This is our space," Charity says.

"I didn't know." The girl's voice comes out dry.

We have her blocked. The only way out that doesn't go through us is the window high on the wall behind her. It's a long way down.

"Did you have a good pee?" Charity asks.

"The way you were banging—" The girl takes a breath. "I thought you wanted to come in and see for yourself."

That makes me laugh. The girl lifts her chin. In profile, in the speckled mirror, she looks proud. Pretty girl in crap clothes. No makeup.

"During break we come in here to smoke," I say. "The first-floor girls' room is where *you* want to be."

"What if I want to smoke?" the girl asks.

"Try Mr. Rossi's room, down the hall," Jacey says. "He's a sweetie. He'll let you, no problem."

She's messing with her. Mr. Rossi would never.

"Got it," the girl says. "Now can I go?"

I lean to a sink and flip the water on. "Wash your hands first."

"Wouldn't want to be unsanitary," Jacey says.

"Pig." From Charity.

The girl's eyes get wide. "Don't call me that."

Charity steps in. "I'll call you whatever."

The girl stumbles from her. "I don't want to be late."

"Then wash," Jacey says.

Time twitches at me. "Hey, I don't want to be late either."

Charity looks at me. "Don't try to stop this."

"I'm not," I say. "But you know Mr. Rossi."

"He'll wait for *you*," she says.

"Shut up."

"Maybe we should go," Jacey says.

"Come on!" Charity's whining. "We've got time."

The girl starts through us. Charity hip-checks her to the sink.

"Wash your damn hands," she says in a voice that would scare me.

The girl stands head down. She takes a shuddery breath.

"I'll fight you. All three. Is that how it is here?"

Charity watches her. Jacey is still.

"This school sucks," I say. "Where are you from?"

"The Bay Area," the girl says. "San Jose. I know how to fight."

Small as she is, it's hard to believe.

"What, you got a knife?" Charity asks.

The girl holds up her hands. "I got claws."

Her nails are short. Unpainted. *No-style*, like the rest of her.

"Is she trying to be funny?" Jacey asks.

"Wash," I tell the girl. "Then we all can leave."

The water's run hot. Steam on the mirror.

"This is my first day at Blue Creek High," the girl says.

"Aww. Poor you," Jacey says.

"Angelyn, *make* her do it," Charity says. "Make her wash her hands."

The first bell goes off. Five minutes to World Cultures.

I stand back. "I'm not being late for this."

"Yeah, let her be dirty," Jacey says.

Charity jabs a finger at the girl. "Watch yourself."

We turn our backs on her.

"Angelyn," the girl says. "You're not Angelyn Stark?"

Jacey and Charity look at each other.

"Yeah, I *am* Angelyn Stark," I say. "You think you know me?"

The girl says no. "But I know someone who does."

I wave my friends out. Charity peeks back. I wait.

"Who knows me?" I ask when we're alone.

The girl walks to the sink, adjusts the temperature, and sticks her hands under.

"My mom is an aide at a nursing home. I was talking with one of the residents, and she said she knew a girl who goes here. You."

I watch her scrub. "I don't know anyone like that."

"Thanks for not letting that girl kill me, by the way."

"I wanted to leave on time. That was it."

She shuts off the water. "Thanks, still. I'm Jeni Traynor."

I shrug.

"I guess we should both leave," Jeni says.

"Wait," I say as she hoists her backpack.

"Don't worry. I won't come in here again."

I shake my head. "What exactly did this *resident* say about me?"

"Well—that you used to be neighbors."

I get cold. "Is her name Mrs. Daly?"

"The residents go by first names, mostly. Hers is Eleanor."

"Eleanor Daly." I nod. "Don't talk to her again."

Jeni blinks. "What?"

"You heard me. Stay away from her."

"But—Eleanor didn't say much, and all I did was listen."

My chest is tight. "All you did was *listen* to crap about me."

"No! She said nice things."

Even worse. "You don't talk to her, you don't talk *about* me. My friends will know if you do, and they'll tell me."

"Those girls?" Jeni shudders. "I wouldn't say a thing around them."

"So why'd you talk to me? I'm the same as they are."

She searches me. "Hey, Angelyn, I'm sorry."

"You will be," I say. Staring.

Jeni takes a step back. "Eleanor said you'd be friendly. Not like this."

I follow. "*This* is me. How I am."

We stop at the wall. She turns her head.

"All right. I'll keep quiet."

"What else did Mrs. Daly say about me?"

"She said— She said you'd had some trouble."

I draw my fist back. "I *am* trouble."

CHAPTER TWO

Out of the girls' room the hall is empty. I take off running, past pink lockers and closed classroom doors until I reach Mr. Rossi's. The late bell is starting as I turn the handle. I'm in as it ends, door shut.

Mr. Rossi stands from his desk. "Ms. Stark, you're late."

"No." I'm breathing hard. "The bell was still ringing."

He looks at the clock. "That's a technicality. If you're late, own it."

I straighten. "I'm not late. It's a technicality if you say I am."

The class moans. Someone laughs. Charity?

Through lowered eyes Mr. Rossi watches me. With a muscled body and blond buzzed hair, he looks more like a jock than a teacher.

"I was not late," I say.

"Lunch detention," he says.

"Mr. Rossi! That's not fair."

"Take your seat, Ms. Stark."

I face the class. "You guys saw. I got here in time. Tell him."

Some kids grin. Others look away. Charity mouths something. At the front of our row, prep-boy Eric takes the time to study *me*.

Mr. Rossi is seated, frowning. "I've made my decision."

"Get me for something I do," I say. "Not this."

"You're holding up class," he says.

"I *can't* have detention. My mom will be so mad."

Mr. Rossi's eyes are icy. Chips of blue.

"Please," I say. Direct to him.

He opens his mouth and shuts it.

What people say about Mr. Rossi is that he's a *hard-ass*. Tough on kids.

But he's young. He hasn't taught long. Maybe he remembers.

"We'll discuss it after class," he says.

I can't tell if I'm in more trouble or less.

"Angelyn, take your seat."

My name. Not *Ms. Stark*. Still, I wait.

Squeaky shoes in the corridor. The noise stops at the classroom door. A knock and the girl from the bathroom—Jeni—steps in.

"Is this World Cultures?" Her voice falls off when she sees me.

"This is World Cultures," Mr. Rossi says. "You're late."

I stare at her. *Not one word.*

"I'm new," Jeni says. "I got lost. I guess."

"You could have asked someone," Mr. Rossi says. "Being new is no excuse."

I leave them. Down the aisle Jacey mimes applause. Charity is grinning. Mr. Rossi gives Jeni the lecture he started with me. The detention part too. I'm guessing that lets me off.

After class I check.

Mr. Rossi shuffles papers. "We're good."

I meet my friends in the hall. I've won and don't know why.

CHAPTER THREE

"It's 'cause he likes you," Charity says when we're on our way to lunch.

I shiver in my stomach. "Does not. He's a teacher."

"Rossi let you out of trouble quick enough," Jacey says.

"It was that girl coming in. That's why."

"Where does she know you from anyway?" Charity asks.

"Nowhere." I walk faster. "She was being stupid. I fixed that."

"You hit her," Jacey says, like she's seen it all before. With me, she has.

I rub a fist against my jeans pocket. "Sure."

We take the sidewalk three across. Girls step off the curb. Guys let us by without giving us shit. It's good to be us.

Lunch is in the back of my boyfriend Steve's truck on the street behind the Agriculture Building. While the boys holler up the block, Jacey, Charity, and I take beers from the cooler and share chips around. Every couple of minutes I check for Steve, pissed at the time he's not spending with me.

"He'll count those cans," I say when Charity reaches for a second one.

"You don't have to tell me!" But she pulls her hand back.

"Angelyn," Jacey says, a spark in her voice. "Your dog is following you again."

I swing around. "What?" And see him. "Shit."

It's Nathan Daly, the Ghost of Blue Creek High, fingers twisted in the hurricane fence that divides the street from Ag, staring at me like I've got his dinner.

I stand, wobbly on my heels. "Go home, dog!"

The girls are laughing.

"Retard," Charity calls.

"Loser," Jacey says.

Nathan doesn't flinch. "Angelyn, I need to talk to you."

"No!" I say so loud it scrapes my throat. My friends stare at me.

I call him the Ghost because I wish he'd disappear.

Steve molds me to the driver's side door, blocking out the daylight, my butt gripped in his hands, my arms around his neck. He kisses me and I taste beer and cigarettes and *him*. I try to forget that Nathan could be watching and that Charity *is*, as she passes beers over the side to Steve's friends. Jacey's up the street with her boyfriend, and I'm wishing mine weren't quite so popular.

"What we need is to be alone," Steve says, an inch from my lips.

I grin. "You read my mind."

With that he pushes off, shooing his friends, ordering Charity from the truck.

I straighten my T. "Wait," I say to no one. Nathan isn't where he was.

Steve comes back, his eyes lit up like Christmas. "Okay, let's go."

"Um." Everybody's watching. Charity looks mad. "Like, where?"

"The reservoir," he says, smile fading. He is big, sandy-haired, good-looking.

"We'd never make it back in time."

Steve taps his fingers along his thigh. "So, today we ditch fifth period."

"I can't. I almost got detention already. Ask Charity."

Charity steps forward. "She did. From Rossi. He barely let her off."

Steve's head is down. "Angelyn, you're not being cool."

I spread a look around the ones watching. Most of them turn.

"Steve." I touch his hand. "I said I couldn't go today. I didn't mean, not ever."

He raises his eyes. "It's been too long."

Dry-mouthed, I nod. "Yes." I'd say anything.

Steve jerks his head to the back of the truck. "We'll have some fun right here."

I roll with Steve in a slow-motion wrestle, my back to his chest, his legs anchoring mine like we're on a toboggan. Empties and half empties rattle and tip around us, splotching my jeans and his from ankle to seat. Steve nips at my neck and runs his hands along my ribs like he's trying to count them. I squirm, breath caught as his fingers spread and stretch. From the street I hear loud talk from the boys and Charity's brassy voice trying to stay even with them.

Steve flips me so I face him, my legs bent between his, his arm around my back, our shoulders to the cab. Covering my mouth with his, he dips his hand to my waist, my stomach, between my thighs, working the denim against me. The rising rhythm takes me and I reach for him, not caring anymore for anything but this feeling between us.

12 The voices blur to a steady hum that's easy to ignore. Until it stops.

I pull my mouth from Steve's, listening.

He presses my hand where it rests on his crotch. "Angelyn—"

"Wait." My voice is ragged.

"Teacher coming," someone says.

My heart beats like a bird's as I struggle to untangle.

"Relax," Steve says, sprawling off. "They never come this far."

"Yeah, and if they do?" I ask, pissed that he can't see it. "The *beer*."

Steve goes white. Possession can get you tossed from Blue Creek High.

I peek over the gate while he crabs for cans, winging them into the cooler.

Charity and the boys are gone. In the auto shop yard that

borders the street, six or seven kids bend and stoop like they're trying to find something. Sacks on their backs.

"It's the lunch detention crew," I say. "Picking trash."

Steve grunts. "I got some cans for them."

In the yard a big boy shifts, and I see the teacher behind him. I duck, I turn, I grab Steve's arm. "Mr. Rossi's with them."

Together we tamp the cooler lid. "Stay down," he says to it, to me, to us.

On our backs I stare at the sky. Cloudless blue.

"Rossi hates me," Steve says. "He has since freshman football."

I snort. "He almost gave *me* detention today."

"Yeah. But he didn't, did he?"

We look at each other, noses close to touching.

The shop gate creaks open to the street.

"Hurry it up." Mr. Rossi's voice.

Steve's throat works. Me, it's hard to swallow.

"We should sit up," I say. "It'll look worse if—"

"Quiet," he says.

Outside, the *scrape scrape* of shoes on asphalt works my nerves as it stops and starts, each time a little closer to where we hide.

Then: "Party down," some guy says.

Steve's eyes look questions at me. I shrug, one-shouldered.

"Whose truck is this?" Mr. Rossi asks.

"Coslow's, I think."

"Steve Coslow's?" Mr. Rossi's voice is sharper. Closer.

Steve is mouthing swears. I curl in like that's going to save us.

His shadow knifes across. Mr. Rossi, looking down.

"Well, what is this?" he says after forever.

"We were just—" I've got nothing else.

Steve lifts himself on an elbow. "Coach, hey. We fell asleep. Is lunch over?"

"Sit up," Mr. Rossi says. "Both of you."

As Steve rises, his arm hits the cooler. The lid slides, settling tilted. I kneel beside him, trying not to look.

Mr. Rossi watches us. Behind him, the detention kids point and grin, whispering things I'm glad that I can't hear. One girl isn't smiling. Jeni, from the bathroom this morning. She's seeing this. I shut my eyes.

"What's the deal?" Steve says. "We were only sleeping."

Mr. Rossi points outside the truck. "Sleeping it off?"

We look. Beer cans around the back tire where the boys stood. Some tipped, others flattened, some nearly full, ready to drink. Souvenirs.

Steve clears his throat. "Those aren't mine. Right, Angelyn?"

"Right." I croak it out.

Mr. Rossi eyes me. "Is this what you do for lunch?"

My face burns. "We're off-campus, Mr. Rossi."

"That excuses nothing. Tell me about the beer."

Steve squeezes my thigh. I put my hand on his.

"I don't know anything about it."

Mr. Rossi takes a step in. The cooler pulses, sending its own light.

"I should have given you detention before."

Steve's fingers twine with mine. His hand is wet.

"Give it to me now," I say.

Mr. Rossi looks off. "Ms. Stark, you come see me after school."

I sink back on my heels. "Okay."

He faces the trash crew. "I need someone to pick up these cans."

Everyone but Jeni finds somewhere else to look.

Mr. Rossi points to her. "Get them, please."

He leads the crew off as Jeni crouches by the truck scooping cans. I'm almost sorry for her. Our eyes meet. The look she gives makes me wish I'd hit her after all.

15

CHAPTER FOUR

I push into the V building as everyone is pushing out. My boot heels ring like gunshots on the steps to the second floor. *You're the best*, Steve said when we were alone. Down the hall to Mr. Rossi's room, I play the words back.

"Come in," he says, like he's been waiting.

I check the clock. "I can't stay long. I have to meet my mom."

Mr. Rossi points to a desk near his. "Sit."

I slide in. "Sorry for whatever."

"I hated seeing you like that," he says.

"Can you just give me the detention?"

"You changed your shirt," Mr. Rossi says.

"Yes," I say, like a question. "I keep an extra in my gym locker."

He stands. "I can still smell it on you."

In shock I watch him start down the length of the board. Erasing.

"Smell what? Mr. Rossi, I do not stink."

He erases some more. "Beer. Did you drink your lunch?"

I've showered. Brushed my teeth.

"No," I say, picking at my jeans.

Mr. Rossi turns. "I saw the cooler. I know *you* didn't bring it."

"If this is about Steve—" I stop.

"You're here and Coslow isn't." He sits on his desk. "Why is that?"

"You told me to come." I work to keep my voice steady.

"You volunteered. He let you do that."

"However it went."

"Give yourself away and you'll have nothing left."

Now I'm squirming. "Tell me what you want me to do."

"Is that what you say to Coslow? During those lunches?"

I stare at him. "What?"

Mr. Rossi curls his lip. "Rolling around in the back of some kid's truck—"

Face burning, I stand. "I'll be there at detention."

"Whoa," he says. "Angelyn, don't take me wrong. Sit. Please."

I bite my lip. And sit.

"You're not in trouble. You don't have detention. I only want to talk."

"About Steve? I won't."

Mr. Rossi moves from his desk to one by me. I stare ahead.

"You're on a path it's hard to turn back from," he says.

"You don't know me to say that."

"I could be wrong. I hope I'm wrong."

I fold my arms. "You are."

"I saw what I saw. But I think you're better than that."

"What makes me better?" I ask.

"You're smart. There's more to you than people know. Am I right?"

"I make C's," I say. "When I'm lucky."

"You could do better," Mr. Rossi says. "Couldn't you?"

I look at him. "In elementary I made A's. Check if you don't believe me."

"I believe you. What was different in your life then?"

"Oh." No one's ever asked. "There was a neighbor lady who helped me with my homework. Mrs. Daly. She used to be a teacher. I'd stop by her place after school."

Mr. Rossi nods. "And? What, she moved?"

I swallow past a sour taste. "Yeah. And I guess I just grew up."

"It's good you had someone like that. Do you now?"

"No," I say.

He taps the desk. "I could help, if you'll let me."

The late-afternoon sun is streaming in, baking the room. I watch the dust dance in the light.

"Why would you want to?"

"I don't know. Maybe because I've been like Coslow."

"Mr. Rossi—"

"And I've been like you. Giving myself up."

I don't know what to say.

"Got ten minutes? I'll tell you about Africa."

"I guess I do. But why Africa?"

He smiles. "That's the unit we're studying in class."

"Oh." I grin. "I knew that."

Mr. Rossi tells me to turn my desk to his. He talks about Africa and AIDS, about the starving people and the economy. He says that his mother was there with the Peace Corps in the 1970s, and he tells me about a trip he made with her when he was only seventeen—*It was beautiful, Angelyn.* I listen to him like I never do in class. I almost forget why I'm here. Almost.

Mr. Rossi asks if I've understood everything.

"Yes," I tell him. "Thanks. I want to travel sometime. And see things."

He motions me up. "Then you will."

We put the desks in line.

"I want to do those things, Mr. Rossi. But I don't know how I can. I'm not going to college or anything. Mom's never been out of state. Neither have I."

"When I was student-teaching in the Bay Area," he says, "I had a student join the Coast Guard. They sent her everywhere. All over the world. She loved it."

"Coast Guard?" First time I've heard those words together.

"I can tell you more another time," he says, back behind his desk.

I gather my stuff. "You'd do that?"

"Sure I would. Now, you will get that homework done."

"I will, Mr. Rossi."

"Okay. I'll be expecting it."

I stop at the door. "The thing with Steve, and the beer—"

He waits.

"It's not what we do every day."

"That's good to know," Mr. Rossi says. "Oh, and, Angelyn?"

"Yes?"

"Tell Genius not to bring that stuff anywhere near school."

"It won't be a problem." I leave smiling.

CHAPTER FIVE

I lied to Mr. Rossi. I don't *have* to meet my mother. Not right away.

After I leave him, I head toward town instead of the bus yard, where Mom works as a dispatcher. Town is three blocks uphill, and I reach the top hungry. Down Main Street I stop at a food cart by the park for a hot dog and Coke. Paying, I see two skate kids watching me while they toe their boards. The bigger boy says something about "boobs," and the smaller one palms his chest. When they see *me* watching *them*, they giggle together like a pair of first-grade girls.

They need to be squelched.

"That isn't cool," I say, down to the bench where the boys are kicking it.

The bigger one fades, but the smaller kid is grinning. "What isn't?" he asks.

"Saying stuff about some girl." I look at each of them. "Some *older* girl."

"Sorry," the big boy says, eyes down.

"You should be."

"What are you going to do with that hot dog?" the little one asks.

Not believing it, I stare. A dirty grin splits his face. The kid is maybe eleven.

"You're too young to know," I tell him.

"You're beautiful. Both of us think so."

"Yeah?" The boys nod. "Go and play with your boards."

The little one starts a spin with his toes. "You going to watch us?"

"I might. If my hot dog gets boring."

The park is small and shaped like a bike wheel, spokes out from a cobblestone center, old oaks and pine trees keeping it shaded. I settle on a bench on the spoke opposite the boys and get to eating.

You're smart, Mr. Rossi said. Mrs. Daly used to say it. That makes two.

The shadows grow long. The skate kids leave. I watch the traffic, keeping an eye out for Mom's truck.

I see Jeni before she sees me, hurrying toward the park from deeper downtown. *Keep going,* I think, but when she stops, I say hey.

Jeni nods from the sidewalk. "Hi." Lukewarm.

Coming in, she takes the bench the boys left.

"You know what time it is?" I call.

Jeni checks her watch. "Quarter to five."

I rub my arms. It's getting cold. I check the traffic. Still no Mom.

"Waiting for someone?" I ask.

She huddles in her jacket. "I think maybe I missed them."

I toss the hot dog wrapper and soda cup in the nearest can and cross to her.

"Tell me about Mrs. Daly."

Jeni is stiff as I sit. "She's in a wheelchair. I don't know why."

"That sucks. Mrs. Daly always liked to garden."

"I think Eleanor's okay for how she is. Just old."

"Not Eleanor," I say. "Mrs. Daly." At Jeni's expression: "That's how I knew her."

Jeni nods. "Mrs. Daly. Okay."

"She was a grandma to me. The only one I knew."

"I miss mine," Jeni says. "It's too far to visit her from here."

"You're from the Bay Area?"

"Oh, you heard that? In the bathroom. I wasn't sure."

"What are you doing downtown anyway?" I ask.

"Exploring," Jeni says. "This place is like a toy town."

I look for Mom's truck. "The same crap happens here as anywhere."

"I guess it does. School today was as bad as at my last one."

"Hey, I didn't know Mr. Rossi would give you detention. Or that you'd be in class with us. He has this thing about kids being late."

"You knew I'd be in *some* class. Late *somewhere.*"

"We're not in the bathroom now. Or at school. Forget that stuff."

Jeni dips her head. "He got you anyway. On the street, with the beer."

"Yeah. He got me. So, call it even?"

"If you want."

We're quiet.

"Come see Mrs. Daly," Jeni says. "I volunteer there on weekends. It's Blue Creek Care Home."

"No. Her grandson wrecked what we had. Years ago. He's a freak."

"Her grandson—Nathan?"

"Yeah." I draw it out. "Nathan Daly. You know him?"

"Nathan's my ride," Jeni says.

"He's coming here?"

She looks confused. "I think Nathan is sweet."

I'm standing, scooping my backpack. "Got to go."

"Wait, Angelyn. What did Nathan do?"

I check the street. Finally, Mom's truck.

"Ask him," I say. Then: "Don't. Nathan lies."

I take off running. And hear him calling: *"Angelyn!"*

Mom's got me spotted. In stopped traffic, she's waving like she's on the *Titanic*. I sprint the rest of the way, settling beside her in a sweaty lump.

"Let's go," I say.

We're stuck.

Mom clears her throat. "That is not who I think it is. It can't be."

"It's not my fault," I say, and see Nathan stopped on the sidewalk, his mouth turned down like some sad clown's.

"Angelyn, it's never your fault."

"Mom, don't blame me! He just showed up."

Her mouth is tight. "You are not to see that boy. Not to talk to him."

"I *know*. Like I'd want to. I hate Nathan worse than anyone."

"Do you hear me?" she says, punching out each word.

"Yes," I say.

Traffic moves. I sit back.

Mom sniffs. "Is that beer I smell?"

My heart beats faster. "Not on me."

She cracks a window.

My stepdad is in the front room, spread along the couch watching baseball. Danny works on-call construction, but no one's called in a while. He doesn't look up as I cut through on the way to my room. Mom follows, and I hear him say, "Hey, Beautiful."

"I ate in town," I call back.

"You're eating with us," Mom says behind me.

Dinner is premade lasagna. I pick while Danny shovels. Mom talks about her job—directing traffic for the whole school, the way she tells it.

"Angelyn screwed up again," she says at the end of one story.

I drop my fork. "Mom, I told you how it was."

She pokes Danny's shoulder. "Hon, you'd be so mad if you knew."

"What was it this time?" he asks.

"Mom," I say, as loud as I dare.

"That boy—the one who used to live next door—Nathan—"

"Mom!" I shout it.

Danny's eyes flick past. "Sherry, you handle it. She's yours."

"Angelyn, you're grounded," Mom says.

She sounds so happy it makes me sick.

CHAPTER SIX

Angelyn, Twelve

From behind the couch, Danny flips the bill of my ball cap down.

"Got you, Angie," he whispers. Mom is still asleep.

"Nuh-uh." I push it up, grinning as he vaults over to join me.

Danny pats the cushions. "Where's the remote?"

I snuggle into my corner. "Sunday mornings I say what's on."

"But—" He flaps his hand at the TV. "This stuff will rot your brain."

MTV. A hip-hop video. The volume, low. "It's my favorite," I say.

Danny folds his arms, but pretty soon he's rapping along, wiggling his hips, dancing on the couch. So stupid I have to laugh.

"You coming to my game?" I ask. "I pitch better when you do."

"You bet I am," he says. "Change the channel, 'kay?"

"With this?" I lift the remote from where I've got it hid.

"Oh, girl. Give it here."

I shake my head. "Nope."

This is our game. Our Sunday-morning game. Mom doesn't
know.

Danny makes puppy eyes. "Please?"

"Well . . ." I hold out the remote.

He reaches. I pull it away.

"Angelyn."

I blink.

"Hand it over." Like he ain't kidding.

This time I send it closer to Danny, unfolding my arm by
inches.

He rubs his fingers like, "Gimme, gimme."

I pull it away again.

He looks at me like he can't believe it.

I lift my shoulders and drop them. Big sigh.

Danny sinks against the couch like he just doesn't care.

I hold the remote like it's my life.

With a low roar he springs at me. I yelp—soft—sliding under
so his arms close on nothing, dropping to the floor to escape. My
bare feet slap linoleum to the kitchen. Danny shuffles behind in a
zombie walk. Down the hall I tiptoe past Mom's room, hand over
mouth, swallowing laughs. Danny's circled back and he's in the
front room before me.

"I'll pass to you," I say, setting my arm like a quarterback's.

Danny fades to the TV, hands up like a wide receiver.

I stretch like the toss will be massive. And stay that way.

"Fake!" I say, breathing out the letters.

He comes at me like a train, slinging an arm around my waist, heaving me to the couch, tumbling after so it's both of us lengthways. I breathe upholstery as Danny grabs for the remote, laughing in the fabric as I hold it to my stomach.

"Angelyn?" someone says. Close.

Danny stops. I shift around. "Oh. Nathan."

Our neighbor stands maybe twenty feet away at the screen door.

Danny rolls off the couch. "Tell him to go."

I sit up slowly. "What do you want, Nathan?"

He holds out a bag of tomatoes. "Grandma sent these."

I smooth my hair. My ball cap is gone. "Leave them on the porch."

"What were you guys doing?" Nathan asks.

"Nothing," Danny says.

"Just go," I say.

He stands there. "Angelyn?"

"What?"

Nathan's face is as red as the tomatoes. "I can see your underwear."

"Oh." My sleep shirt is ridden to my waist. I tug at it, hating him.

Danny passes me. "I'll take the tomatoes."

Nathan peeks around when he opens the door. "Angelyn, you okay?"

"Yes," I say, like, DUH!

Danny reaches for the bag and latches the screen door shut.
He pushes the front door closed. He sets the tomatoes on an end
table.

"That kid's not right."

I check Mom's room. Her door is shut, still.

Danny comes to the couch. "Scoot."

I sit at one end, him at the other.

"What was that about?" he asks.

"Nathan's real dumb at school."

"He likes you, huh?"

"Yuck! No."

30

"Well, he's seen you like that," Danny says.

I curl my legs under. Hide my face.

"You didn't do anything wrong," he says.

"Nathan acted like I did."

"So what on him, and, no, you didn't."

I peek at Danny. He's looking over real serious.

"Kiddo, I don't want you to feel funny, or bad, or—"

"I feel good with you."

"Yeah?" He smiles. "Me too."

"I guess Nathan will tell everyone he saw my pants." I try to
laugh.

"That's all, if we're lucky."

"Huh?"

"Maybe we're in trouble," Danny says. "He could tell any lie."

"What lie? I won't let him."

He rubs a thumb over his lips. "We're friends, right?"

"Yeah, we're friends." I'm scared.

"Friends back each other up," he says.

Mom's door creaks open. "Was someone here?" she says, yawning.

I've still got the remote. I slide it to Danny across the cushions.

"Just now." She steps into the room. "I thought I heard—"

Danny looks at me, and me at him.

"Nothing," he says.

"Nobody," I say.

CHAPTER SEVEN

Next Morning,
Sidewalk in Front of Ag

Steve doesn't believe me. "Rossi was okay about the beer?"

I sway with him, my hands on his on my hips.

"Don't bring it to school was all he said."

Steve says, "Not a problem."

"That's what I told Mr. Rossi."

He pulls me to him. "Sweet."

Nearby, Jacey is wound around JT. Other couples hold each other along the walk, the unattached ones teasing across from boy/girl groups. This is our place before school. My place with Steve. Thirtysome of us gather. *Hicks*, the others call us. The prep kids, the rich kids, the jocks. Or, *cowboys*. The words don't fit everyone. They sure don't fit me. Steve's family runs cattle. So does JT's. Jacey and Charity live on ranch land—neighbors—but their dads are in real estate.

Me, I'm here because I'm friends with them and because last year Steve decided that he liked me.

Fine, hot girl, he called me then.

Cowboy Steve, I called him.

"Mom grounded me," I say against his lips.

Steve stands back. "Because of the beer?"

On tiptoe, in his ear: "Mr. Rossi didn't tell. She's just being a bitch."

He curves his hands around my butt. "Reservoir today then for sure."

I wiggle so I face front. "I don't know."

He presses against me. "You can't get any more grounded than you are."

I stare at the ball field across the street, empty but for birds hunting breakfast.

"I can't get any more grounded," I say.

"Ms. Stark," Mr. Rossi says as I walk into World Cultures with the girls.

"Hey." I stop smiling when I see yesterday's homework on the board.

Jacey stops at his desk. "Say hi to *us*, Mr. Rossi."

Charity crowds next to her. "Yeah. You see us too."

"I do," he says. "Hello, girls."

I push them on.

When we're in our desks: "Did you do the homework?" I ask.

Charity says, "No." Jacey shakes her head.

"I didn't either. I said I would. I'm screwed."

"Yeah, by him," Charity says.

■ ■ ■

Mr. Rossi stops me when class is over.

"No homework?" he asks, pointing to the pile on his desk.

"Sorry, Mr. Rossi. I was fighting with my mom."

"Bad excuse, Angelyn. Take your own responsibility."

In the doorway the girls laugh. I send them a death stare.

"Keep your focus," Mr. Rossi says.

"I'll get you the work. I promise."

"You said that before, and it didn't happen."

I flinch. "I'll give you yesterday's homework and today's. Tomorrow."

Mr. Rossi leans back in his chair.

"I will! I wrote the assignments down."

"Fool me once," he says.

"You have to believe me." My voice shakes.

At the Reservoir

"People think I suck," I say on Steve's lap. "Everybody's pissed."

"I'm not. Gelly." Hands in my hair, he pulls my face to his.

A blast of wind rattles the truck, breaking our kiss. We're ten miles from school, alone in the stadium-sized parking lot overlooking the water.

"Gelly." I make a lemon face. "That is so . . . yuck."

"Don't tell anyone I call you that."

"I won't." I shift against him. "Cowboy Steve."

He runs a finger along my cheek. "Let's get in back."

I sit up, the steering wheel against me. "No. It's too windy outside."

Steve slides me off his lap. "So, we'll keep our heads down."

Scrambling to my knees, I lean in for a kiss, my hands braced on his thighs.

"You're trying to change the subject," he says, though I haven't said a thing.

My hands drift downward. "We can do enough in the cab."

"I want to stretch out." He sounds about six years old.

I run my nails along his fly. "I'll do better in here."

"You want to get out of doing stuff." His voice fades as I undo the buttons.

"I am doing stuff." I look up. "Want me to stop?" Gently, I work him free.

Steve says nothing. He groans.

Afterward he thanks me like a little boy.

"Kiss me, then," I tell him, playing tough. He does it.

Neither of us has much to say after that. It's hot in the truck. Close.

"I'm getting out," I say, opening my side.

Steve opens his. "See, now it's not too windy for you."

Outside he buttons up. I walk to the edge of the lot overlooking the water. It's gray and rocking today, more ocean than lake.

He joins me. Puts his arm around me. It feels good underneath.

"You know something?" Steve says. "I am pissed with you."

I check him. "What'd I do?"

"It's what you don't do. And you know what I mean."

"I have." I walk away, elbows clasped.

He follows. "Twice we've done it. I hardly remember the last time."

"Lie number one." The wind whips my hair in my face, my eyes.

Steve grins. "Okay. May 28. Here. Four months ago, Angelyn."

I shrug. "I didn't see you over the summer."

"You told me not to come around."

I hold my hair back with both hands. "My mom doesn't trust me."

"As much as everyone thinks you party—"

"Oh, everyone *who*? What does that mean?"

He looks off. "Forget it."

In the truck I sit, arms folded, staring out the side.

"Don't be like that," Steve shouts as we tear across the lot.

"Who's been talking about me? You?"

"JT and Jacey are doing it. You don't talk to her about me?"

"No." It's true. I don't.

"I guess you're better than me, then."

He swings onto the road out.

"It's great how you save this for *after* I do my thing."

"You were acting so pure," Steve says. "I get tired of it."

"Pure?" I look at his crotch. "Didn't taste that way to me."

He snorts. "Okay, so you're talented. You know I want more."

"Most guys would be glad for what you get."

"Conceited, much?" He downshifts for the climb to the highway.

I touch his arm. "Let's not do this again."

Steve twitches me off. "You think I don't know it's how you keep me away?"

"I don't keep you away. I'm here. Doesn't that count?"

He's frowning. "You're not on it like a girlfriend should be."

The reservoir disappears as we round a curve into thick brush.

"I'm sick of it, Angelyn."

I watch him. "Another time, I will. I promise."

"Your hand," he says. "Your mouth—"

"Stop it."

"Could be *anybody's* hand, or mouth."

"Right." I'm squirming.

Steve looks over. "I want you, Angelyn. I want us to want each other."

"We do," I say. No color to it.

"Look. Whatever you're afraid of, or think you are—"

"I'm not *afraid* of anything." It comes out vicious.

He lifts his hands and slams them on the wheel. The truck fishtails, and for a scary second he fights for control.

"Watch it," I say, wishing I didn't after.

"We are never getting together again. Is that what you're saying?"

"Another time, I said."

Steve jerks the truck to a stop.

"What?" I ask, hands against the dashboard.

"I'll call your bluff right here. We skip the afternoon. Circle back to the lot. We'd have two hours before school's out."

"No," I say. He hisses something. "They'd get us both for cutting. Mom grounded me last night. I can't get into trouble again that fast."

"All excuses."

I check the dashboard clock. "Lunch'll be over. We should go."

"You *act* so pure. And I know you're not."

"Okay, you said that before. What does it mean?"

Steve stares ahead.

"If I'm dirty like that, maybe you don't want me in your truck."

"Maybe I don't."

I catch my breath. "Are we supposed to sit here until I give in?"

No answer from him.

"Not today, Steve. I didn't mean today. It doesn't make sense, today."

He flexes his fingers. "Uh-huh."

We sit unmoving. I watch the clock and wrench from it.

"What do you care as long as you get off? It's all the same, isn't it? Once it's done."

Steve clears his throat. "It's not the same. One kind is, you're with me."

"It's a damn chore," I say. Mostly to myself.

"Get out." He's quiet.

"What?"

Steve says it again—shouts it: "GET OUT."

I get out.

He drives away.

CHAPTER EIGHT

I watch the truck blast around a corner.

Gone.

"I can't believe this," I say. To no one. I don't like the way I sound. Weak.

"Bastard," I add, with a kick to the pavement.

It's a mile or more to the highway, uphill in winding turns through thick brush. A mile back to the parking lot and the cool breeze off the water. Here the air doesn't move. I swirl my hair in a topknot and let it drop, heavy on my shoulders. I am already sweating.

I start the climb, hobbling on asphalt in boots meant for show. My shirt clings like a second skin. By the time I reach the curve where the truck disappeared, it's sweated through.

"*Hate* you," I say, coming out of the turn to the next identical stretch of road.

Around another curve I follow a break in the brush to a picnic area I've never noticed. There's a restroom, a pay phone bolted to its side. A few tables. A barbecue pit. A hip-high faucet in a circle of gravel. I head for it.

The water is rusty. Lukewarm. I let it run cool and duck my head under, the water sluicing my face as I drink. As I stand, weeds move in the woods beyond the restroom. It's like someone's grabbed my throat.

"Who's there?"

A yip comes back, choked as my question, and a medium-sized dog after it, bursting through the brush, curved tail wagging, covered with burrs.

I exhale hard. I have to pee.

The dog is at the bathroom door when I come out.

"Go home," I say, without much heat, taking a closer look.

It's black with brown spots, its body as matted as its tail. A spaniel mix, maybe, with floppy ears. It watches with bright brown eyes.

"I guess you won't kill me. I hope you're not contagious."

Its tail wags harder.

I kneel on the concrete. "Come here." The dog does. I pet it—her—the rough fur scraping my skin. So many burrs.

"Somebody dumped you." And then I start to cry.

The dog drinks from the faucet while I sit at a table thinking what to do next. The pay phone juts like an ear off the restroom structure. I can't call my mom. *Would not* call Danny. I have no money for a cab, and it's not like they'd come here anyway.

Steve is the only one I could call.

The dog trots over and sits at my feet.

I lift her to the bench. "Who left you here?"

Campers, I'm guessing. Late-summer campers with less room leaving the reservoir than they had coming in.

"People suck." I work a sticker from the tangled fur behind her ear.

In the distance, a honk. More honks, coming in.

"I will kill him," I say. Pissed that I'm happy.

The dog strains against my hands, wanting *DOWN*. I let her go.

Between honks Steve is shouting my name. The dog takes off like he's calling her. I follow, thinking what I'll say to him.

The truck slides around the corner as I step out of the clearing. The dog is down the road, safe in a patch of weeds. I fold my arms and wait for Steve to see me.

He skids past, jams on the brakes, and reverses to where I stand.

"Get in," he says. No eye contact.

The dog tears for the truck, barking nonstop.

"Asshole," I say over her.

Steve waves an arm. "Let's go."

The dog crouches at his door. Gathering herself, she jumps, falling in a scrape of nails.

"Hey," Steve shouts. "Dolly, back!"

I stare at him. "What did you call her?"

The dog jumps again. Falls again, whimpering.

Steve revs the engine. "Angelyn, come on!"

"Dolly?" I say to him. To her: "Dolly?"

The dog is watching me. I walk to her, fingers outstretched. She skitters off.

"Steve," I say, "do you know this dog?"

"No," he says. "Now hurry."

I smooth my shirt. "I think you do." My stomach trembles.

Steve does a half-assed finger snap. "We can make it if we leave now."

"You dumped her. Didn't you? Whose is she?"

His jaw works. "Forget the dog and come with me."

I look at Dolly. "What will happen to her?"

Steve says, "It's just a dog."

Head tilted, Dolly treads beside the truck.

"How could you do that?" I ask.

"Do you want to get back to school or don't you?"

"It's not right," I say slowly.

Steve turns. "Angelyn, I will leave without you. Think I won't? You can find your own way back and I won't know a thing about it. I was never here."

I believe him. I get in.

"It's my sister's dog," Steve says on our way back. "Some mutt she found at college. She left it with us, and my folks said, *Get rid of it.* What was I supposed to do?"

"Don't know," I say, tracing a pattern in the circle I've breathed on the window.

"A ranch isn't some playground for animals. It's a business."

43

"Nice quote. Who said it first, your mom or your dad?"

"I left food." Steve is whining. "It's better than the Pound, yeah?"

"Yeah. You're a real great guy."

"Stop giving me crap. I didn't have a choice!"

I look at him. "You dumped *me* like you dumped that dog."

Steve wags a finger. "I came back for you."

"Thanks!" I say with a fake sweet smile.

"All right, I'll say it: Sorry. I shouldn't have left you."

Close to campus, we pass the bus yard where my mom works.

I duck. Steve grabs my neck and squeezes.

"While you're down there . . . ," he says in his Sex voice.

I twist from him and slide across the vinyl.

"Hey!" Steve says. "I'm only playing."

I hug the door. "Well, I'm not."

"Ange, I said I was sorry. What more do you want?"

I feel like crying. "Go back for her."

"The dog?" He shakes his head. "And do what?"

"Stand up for her. Tell your parents how it's going to be."

"Yeah, that'll happen."

We speed past Ag. I see a few of our friends still there.

"We got back in time," Steve says. "Told you."

I'm shaking, I'm so pissed. "What was all that about me being pure?"

He sighs. "Let's don't go there."

"*You* went there. Now tell."

"All right. Seventh, eighth grade, I heard you'd do anything."

"And anyone?" I ask after a moment.

He eyes me. "Yeah. It's what I heard."

We turn onto School Street. Steve scans for parking.

"People running their mouths," I say. "You shouldn't have believed them."

"Some of it had to be true. Too many people said."

He puts the truck in neutral and coasts into a spot by the pool.

"What exactly are you talking about?" I'm thinking of Nathan's lies.

"I don't know. You and Jacey—" Steve is grinning.

"I kissed her at a party. Eighth grade. On a dare."

His grin broadens. "Pretty hot. I heard other stuff happened at those parties."

On safer ground, I shrug. "Guys have always liked me. So? You did too."

"I like you right now, Angelyn. You're juicy, is what you are."

"Juicy?"

"That's a good thing. Trust me." He reaches for my leg.

I pull it away. "No."

The engine ticks cool as we sit in the truck. Outside, the pool shimmers. Beyond it I can see a corner of the football field and the bleachers built into the hill that overlooks the school.

"We'll miss the bell," Steve says. Neither of us moves.

"You know it's wrong about the dog."

"It's sad, yeah, but that's the way things go sometimes."

"Steve. It didn't just happen. You did it."

He leans over. "Subject *done*."

I let him kiss me. "One of our friends could take her, maybe."

"Forget the damn dog."

I sit back. "You brought me there. You brought her there."

"Not the same, Angelyn. It's a big place."

"All the time you're thinking about this *stuff* that people said about me."

"I can't help that," Steve says. "Any guy would."

"*Talking* about me with JT and whoever else—"

"That's just normal."

I pop the door. "Mr. Rossi was right about you."

Steve takes my arm. "What did you say?"

"It's what *he* said." Pulling free. Out of the truck. "You're no good for me."

"Hang on." He slides out after me. "Coach said that? What did you say back?"

I look up at him. "Nothing! I stood up for you."

Steve studies me. "You did?"

My face is tight, the start of a sunburn. "Yeah. What you won't do for me."

"Now stop that." He sounds as pissed as he did at the reservoir.

The bell rings, a distant sound. I duck around him.

Steve follows. "Are you breaking up with me?"

I haven't thought it, haven't put it in words, but: "Yeah. I am."

"Over *this*?" he says. "You are not."

My boots and Steve's clatter on the cobblestone path by the pool.

"You don't want me anyway," I say.

"I think you got that backward."

"You get *rid* of me if I don't do what you want. Like you got rid of that dog."

"*Once*," Steve says. "Once. How many times do I got to say, *Sorry*?"

I walk faster. "Not ever again, because we are through."

"I have been good for you. I took you on no matter what my friends said."

I look to the sky. "You took me on *because* of what they said. Didn't you?"

"Angelyn, I always respected you! Tell me once when I didn't."

"Our first time I was *drunk*."

"Not that drunk," Steve says.

I cut across to the lawn between the pool and the band room.

"You've got nowhere to go," he says behind me. "All your friends are mine."

"Not Jacey and Charity."

Steve laughs. "Those two skanks? They'd go with me."

I check him. "You're wrong."

"Want to test it?"

We stare at each other.

The second bell rings. "Great," I say.

Steve waves me in. "We're late anyway. Come on. We'll work this out."

I walk backward away. "Good luck finding someone—*juicy*—as me."

"You'll end up with that retard. Yeah. You and him, together forever."

He's never mentioned Nathan. "What are you talking about?"

"That blond kid who follows you around. Maybe you'll fuck him."

"Anyone but you." My voice cracks. "*Anyone.* Dog dumper."

"That's it." Steve digs in for a run, arms pumping.

I turn, heels slipping, hard into the arms of Mr. Rossi.

CHAPTER NINE

Hands on my arms, Mr. Rossi sets me back gently.

"What is this?" he asks. Behind him, a handful of kids rush along the fenced corridor between the creek and the foreign-language portables, bolting into whichever is theirs.

I don't know what to say.

Mr. Rossi studies me. "Angelyn?"

My smell registers: BO for real. I plaster my arms to my sides.

Steve pulls up. "Hey, Coach. We're just trying to get to class on time."

Mr. Rossi says, "You're both late, and I don't have time to deal with it."

"We'll be on our way," Steve says.

"I'm not going anywhere with you," I say.

"Ms. Stark, are you all right?" Mr. Rossi asks.

I give an automatic answer. "Sure."

"Angelyn got a little hot," Steve says. "Now we're good."

I sigh, nothing more.

"Coslow, are you a hasty dresser?"

Steve says, "Huh?" Mr. Rossi points down.

I see it with Steve—the buttons one-off along his fly. Hand to mouth, I laugh.

Steve covers himself. "Funny."

I lose the smile. What Mr. Rossi must think.

"Can I get a late pass to PE?" I ask.

"I need one too," Steve says. "For Welding."

"I don't like the two of you together," Mr. Rossi says.

Steve looks at me. "Tell him we're okay."

"Shut up." I manage not to scream it.

"Well, you stupid—" He bites down hard.

Mr. Rossi breaks the quiet. "Coslow, get to Welding."

"Without a pass?" Steve asks.

"Yeah. Go. Lunch detention tomorrow," he calls after.

Steve misses a step.

Mr. Rossi smiles at me. "I'll write you that pass. Then I have to leave."

All I can do is nod.

"Angelyn, Coslow didn't hurt you?"

I bite my lip. "No."

Through a propped door I hear my old Spanish teacher, Mrs. Tierney, taking roll with a twist.

"Estefani Adalia," she calls. "Stephanie Noble, I mean *you*."

"Mrs. Tierney called me 'Angelita' when I was in there," I say. "*AHN-hell-ita*. 'Little Angel.' Guys would laugh."

"Guys are idiots," Mr. Rossi says.

"I guess she wasn't that swift either. Teachers don't usually like me."

He points me over to the picnic area. "Now, what is going on?"

In direct sunlight I squint at him. "I thought you had to go."

"It's my free period," Mr. Rossi says. "I spend it how I want."

I tell him about the dog. What it was like, stuck with her, waiting.

"Steve came back for me. Not her. He wants me to thank him for it."

Mr. Rossi rubs his chin. "That stinks he put you through that."

"She'll die out there. I know she will. It'll kill me thinking about it."

"I could call someone. Animal Control. Coslow's parents."

"They told him to do it. And the Pound is no place for Dolly."

"I don't know what to tell you, kiddo."

That word—*kiddo*. "Somebody used to call me that."

Mr. Rossi asks, "Who?"

I shake my head. "Isn't there *anything*—?"

"I could . . . I suppose . . ." He trails off.

"Help her?" I focus on him. "Would you, Mr. Rossi?"

He shifts in the grass. "I'd like to, sure. But how?"

"If you went out there, she'd come to you. I know she would."

"And then what? I adopt the dog? It's not so easy."

"All she needs is a chance."

"My life is not my own," Mr. Rossi says. "I have a wife. A son."

News to me. His family. "They might like a dog. Your son would."

He sighs. "Can *you* take the dog? Would your parents—"

"My mom? I don't think so. My stepdad? No."

"Why is this so important to you?"

Gooseflesh rises as I tell him the truth: "I know what it's like to be left."

Something plays over Mr. Rossi's face. I stare at him, wishing, willing, *hoping.*

He looks away. "I'm sorry."

I breathe out. "You won't help."

"I wish I could. Honestly."

"Mr. Rossi, you can. You have a car, right? You said you had the time."

"Angelyn. No."

"The truth is, you don't want to. You don't think she's worth it."

He looks at me again. "Hey."

I turn. "I don't need a pass."

Mr. Rossi says, "Wait."

"Why?" I ask.

"Because. All right. Let's go on out and get her."

Next to him in the family car, I can't quite believe where I'm at.

We don't talk except for my directions to the place.

Dolly is sitting where Steve stopped the truck.

"She would have waited forever." My heart hurts at the thought.

Mr. Rossi parks. "That's the dog?"

I see her through his eyes, ragged, dirty, and not very petlike.

"She's a great dog." I pile out of the car.

Dolly stands. Her tail wags when I call, but she doesn't come. I walk at her, and she dances back with a sad yap.

Crouching, I croon.

Dolly's ears perk.

I click my tongue. She takes a few steps in.

I say her name, gently as I know how.

Dolly comes closer.

I curl my fingers. "Here, babe."

With that she barks, running at me on stumpy legs that pick up speed. She jumps past my hand, knocking me to my butt. I hold Dolly close, laughing as she licks my chin, the asphalt hot against my jeans.

"Angelyn!"

I look around. Mr. Rossi is out of the car, grinning.

Inside I hold as much of Dolly on my lap as I can.

"Sorry about the mess," I say, her muddy paws spilling over.

"I know about mess," Mr. Rossi says. "I have a small kid."

His car smells new. The carpet is crumbless.

"Thanks," I say. "For everything."

He touches Dolly's head. Against me, her heart beats wildly.

"I think you're right. She'll make a good pet."

"Why are you being so nice?" I ask.

Quiet rises. Mr. Rossi starts the car.

"What were you doing out here with Coslow? Or should I guess?"

I stare ahead. "I won't be doing it anymore."

"Good," he says.

We drive past the high school, through town, and out of it. Onto a country lane through forested pastureland. The trees go on for miles.

"You're a long way from everything," I say.

Mr. Rossi grunts.

The woods thin and I see houses behind them. Big houses on large lots down curving driveways. Privacy hedges and high fences block some from view. Mr. Rossi turns in at a drive like that, under a white iron arch, a prancing horse at its center. We rumble down a gravel drive through tall oaks and towering oleander. I look around and I can't see the road.

"Mr. Rossi, are you bringing me here to do something to me?"

"What?" He slows the car. "No, Angelyn. No."

I fiddle with Dolly's ears. "I was wondering."

"I'm not like that," he says.

Around a bend I see the house. Two stories, sparkling white with a wraparound porch. An inground pool and vegetable garden on the left. On the right, a stand-alone garage and a tire swing hanging from a thick-limbed oak.

"This is your place? It looks like something on TV."

"Just an updated farmhouse," Mr. Rossi says.

"You're rich." Hyperaware of my beat-down clothes, my sweaty body.

"My family was, maybe. Not me."

I look at him. "You grew up here?"

"Yeah. Local boy makes good."

I don't know if I'm supposed to smile at that. Mr. Rossi isn't smiling.

"So, you know what it's like to be a kid here," I say.

"Sure." He glances over. "It wasn't all that long ago."

"Isn't it weird, teaching where you went?"

"It's a job," Mr. Rossi says, "but I never thought I'd end up back here."

He parks a good way from the house, opposite the tire swing.

"Is your wife around?" I ask.

"What do you mean by that?" Mr. Rossi speaks sharply.

I pick my words. "I thought you had to check with her. About Dolly."

"No, that's all right. Wait in the car."

When he's gone, Dolly rises off my lap, whimpering.

"Don't worry," I say. "He'll be back."

She digs her blunt nails in my thighs, staring up.

"Oh! Bathroom." I open the door fast.

Dolly dives to the ground. She noses in the grass and squats.

I have to go too.

Mr. Rossi comes out of the house hands full, a couple of soup bowls in one, a dusty-looking collar and leash in the other.

"Hey. I thought you were going to stay in the car."

I shift my weight. "Dolly had to go."

"Okay." He comes down the steps. "I got some stuff to get her started."

"Mr. Rossi, I do too. Have to go, I mean."

He stares at me. "I'm not letting you in the house."

That hurts. "Why not? If no one's home."

"It's not a good idea."

"But—" I wave my hand.

"All right." Not happy. "Use the one downstairs, off the hall."

Embarrassed, I edge past. "Thanks."

Inside the house it's cool and dim, blinds down in the living room. I find the bathroom easily, gleaming clean in shades of peach and black, claw-foot tub standing out from the wall. Like something from TV—again.

A woman's silky yellow tank hangs from the shower rod. When I'm done, I check the size. Medium. My size. From a pile on a wicker holder, I take a couple of towels. I wash the grit from my face and clean under my arms, rinsing the towels afterward. I pick burrs and twigs off my T, eyeing the clean and beautiful shirt on the hanger.

"Angelyn!" Mr. Rossi calls down the hall. "What are you doing in there?"

"Almost done," I say through caught breath. "Can I borrow a shirt?"

"Of course you can't," he says, louder than he needs to. "Come on!"

I leave the wet towels curled in the sink for him to explain.

He's on the porch. Dolly's leashed to a clothesline off the garage, her whole body wagging as she inhales what's in the bowl.

"Thanks for helping her," I say.

Mr. Rossi locks the door.

"Did you used to have a dog?" I ask on our way down the steps.

He doesn't answer.

As he starts the car: "I took a risk," Mr. Rossi says.

"I know," I say. "I meant it when I thanked you."

"I hope I did the right thing."

My mouth is dry. "You did."

"If you told the wrong person. Said it the wrong way."

"Mr. Rossi, I'm not saying anything to anyone."

We bump along through shadows of tree and brush.

"I'm sorry I snapped at you," he says. "It all just came at me."

Sorry? I smile. "That's okay. I'll get a clean shirt from my gym locker."

"I'll write you that pass when we get back," Mr. Rossi says.

"You're not like a teacher."

"Um, thanks?" he says.

"You rescued us. Dolly and me. I won't forget that."

"The way you cared about that dog, you got me to care."

"She will be okay? At your house, with your family?"

"Yes." He says it like he means it.

I sit back. "Good."

"Hey, Angelyn. On the way in you asked if I brought you here to hurt you."

I look over. "I didn't say it like that."

"No, I'm glad you asked. *I* didn't have bad intentions, but somebody else might have. Be careful where you put your trust, all right?"

"Mr. Rossi, I'm not afraid of you."

"It's not about being afraid," he says. "It's about being aware."

I'm staring. *Aware of what?* I want to ask, but I keep still.

CHAPTER TEN

Mom pulls up to the drive-through window. "I heard you late."

I'm yawning. "Homework."

She hands me my chocolate and takes her coffee.

"Are you falling behind?"

I inhale the sweet steam. "More like moving ahead."

Near the high school I remember about Steve.

"Mom! Drop me by the auditorium, okay?"

She swings a left. "Not Ag?"

"No." A twinge in my stomach.

"Well, I won't bother to ask why."

I face the window. "You don't want to know why."

Mom pulls to the curb. "I don't have time for stories."

Cold and dark. I sigh getting out.

"Why do we have to come to school so stupid early?"

"Because *I* do," she says. "Take the bus sometime if you don't like it."

"Okay, then." We both know it's not happening.

"You're welcome," Mom says as I stand by the door.

"Thanks," I say, closing it short of a slam.

Ninety minutes to the bell.

I cross to the Humanities Building in a kind of hanging mist and clatter up metal stairs lit by reflectors.

"Hi," someone says, and I grip the rail. It's wet.

"Gross," I say, then, "Hey."

Jeni is sitting on the top step.

"What are you doing here?" I ask, climbing slower.

"Waiting for class," she says. "Is this place off-limits too?"

"Off-limits? No."

"Your friends aren't coming?"

"They don't know I'm here."

Jeni eyes me as I step past into the outside corridor. I stop three doors down, at my English classroom.

"I'm waiting for school to start, just like you are. Here, just for today."

Some tension leaves her shoulders.

"*Your* friend isn't coming, is he? Nathan?"

"Nathan delivers papers before school," Jeni says. "He dropped me off."

I move to the rail. "Boy, I can't see it. You and him."

"I'm not with Nathan," she says. "You've got that wrong."

"No?" I say, stretching.

Jeni points between us. "Can I—?"

Curious, I nod.

She comes over. "We're staying with them. My mom and me."

"You're staying with Nathan and his dad?"

Jeni kicks at the tar paper. "It's complicated."

I look out at the field. "Must be."

"My mom and his dad are seeing each other. Dating, I guess."

"Huh."

"Yeah."

"Does Nathan's dad still look like Bigfoot?" I ask.

Jeni laughs. "My mom is picky like that."

I grin. "Probably about as picky as mine."

Jacey and Charity are talking close when I walk into the bath-room at break. They split apart like a cheating couple, Charity's words left hanging—

... *cut her off.*

I cross to them. "Hi."

Jacey looks away.

"Got a smoke?" I ask.

She fumbles in her purse and hands me one.

I wave the butt under Charity's nose. "How about a light?"

She slaps it away. *"Wait."*

And flips a matchbook at me like a tiny Frisbee.

It bounces off my chest, hits the tiles, and skids under a sink.

I crumple the cigarette. "What's going on?"

"Steve is talking bad about you," Charity says.

"Really bad," says Jacey.

"Oh." I wait. "And you guys are listening?"

"Angelyn, he is *pissed.*" Jacey is wide-eyed.

"That's his problem," I say.

"Where were you this morning?" She's close to a whisper.

"Here. School. Just nowhere near Steve. I'm done with him."

"Done with him? Why didn't you call last night and tell me?"

"I don't call! You know I don't. Not with *them* listening."

The girls look at each other.

"What is Steve saying?" I ask.

"That you screwed him over," Jacey says. "Got him detention."

"*I* did? It was all Steve."

"*Slut, bitch, whore*," Charity recites. "He called you that."

"All that?" They nod. "And you guys told him off—right?"

Charity makes a face. "Oh, right, Angelyn."

"No one could have stopped him," Jacey says.

For a second—a second—I feel like crying.

"You're a pair of pussies," I say.

Charity smiles. "Steve told us to take a break from you."

I stare at her. "So you *are*?"

"JT and Steve are tight," Jacey says. "I have to respect that."

"*Respect* it? They talk crap about you, Jace. Did you know?"

"Angelyn, don't put me in the middle."

"We should go," Charity says. Adding, "Jacey."

"Not me?" Like I'm shocked.

The girls march out.

I check myself.

My hair hangs right. My shirt fits better than either of theirs.

Way better.

The hurt on my face is easy to read. They must have read it.

It kills me that Steve was right.

Before class. Mr. Rossi reads the newspaper at his desk. The girls talk about a party for Jacey's baby sister. Who's coming. Who's bringing what. I take my notebook out and draw connecting circles. I'm banned from both their houses, but usually they don't throw it in my face.

Jeni looks over a couple of times from across the room.

The bell rings.

"Homework," Mr. Rossi says.

I pull mine out, folded, from the text. A double assignment like I said.

"What is she doing?" Charity asks, like *eww*.

Mr. Rossi walks to our row. "Did you do the homework, Ms. Flint?"

"Sure," Charity says. "I left it at home by accident."

"Same here," Jacey says. "Can we bring ours tomorrow?"

Front row, Eric is turned and grinning.

"Hey, if we *have* ours, do we get extra credit?"

"No one's talking to you," I say out of reflex.

He whips around.

"Ms. Stark, you have your work?" Mr. Rossi is casual.

I smooth the papers. "Yes."

He nods. "Good girl." And walks away.

I can't believe he said it.

"That is so not cool," Charity says.

But someplace inside I'm glad he did.

There's a quiz. Same stuff that was in the homework.

Mr. Rossi calls time. "Exchange papers."

"Jacey, give me yours," Charity says. "Here's mine."

Usually, the three of us switch.

Mr. Rossi lifts his clipboard. "Everyone set?"

"Angelyn needs a partner!" Charity calls.

I look around. "Hey."

Jeni has her hand up. "Can we correct our own?"

"You girls trade," Mr. Rossi says.

We meet at the center of the room. Jeni smiles, handing me her quiz.

"Look at her *shoes*," Charity says.

I check mine. I'm wearing boots. She doesn't mean me.

Jeni's got on shapeless tennies with gray laces. They've seen some miles.

"What a bitch, huh?" she whispers.

I study Jeni's shoes. "Girl, you know how to accessorize."

Charity cackles. Jacey laughs. Scattered others too, throughout the room.

Jeni puts one foot behind the other, hiding nothing.

"Sit down, you two." Mr. Rossi, like he's disappointed.

I don't even know why I said it.

When we call scores, I've made an A. So has Jeni.

Jacey and Charity fail.

At the bell Jeni bolts. The girls leave ahead of me, talking at a clip. As I step into the hall, Mr. Rossi calls after me.

I look back, but we're cut off by the crowd changing classes. I push through to a spot against the wall.

He stands in the doorway, hand up in the A-OK sign.

Thinking it's about the quiz, I nod.

Kids stream between us. Next time there's a gap, Mr. Rossi pats the air by his thigh.

"*The dog,*" he mouths.

Then I get it. Dolly is okay. Whatever Steve or anyone says, I did good.

Smiling, I lean against the wall. I hold the smile until Mr. Rossi can see it.

The crowd splits as I move down the stairs. At the landing I see why—

Nathan in the middle, searching faces. His eyes light up when he sees mine.

"Angelyn! Hey."

Shaking my head, I point to the window.

Out of traffic, I tell him, "Nathan, you have got to stop."

He leans in with a shaky smile. "I only want to—"

"Ask me out? No, like never. Go away."

"Talk, Angelyn. I only want to talk."

"Well, I *don't.*"

"It's about Grandma." His voice catches.

"That girl Jeni said she was all right." My voice is distant in my ears.

"Jeni doesn't know her like she was before."

"There's nothing about—*before*—that I want to remember."

"Angelyn, you have to come see her! You have to come *now.*"

I step back into the stream and let it carry me from him.

CHAPTER ELEVEN

At lunch I leave the classroom building with nowhere to go. But the girls are waiting at the usual place, the footbridge over Blue Creek.

"We're not fighting?" I ask, walking up.

Charity grins. "That was funny about her shoes."

"Thanks," I say. Icy.

"It's dumb to fight," Jacey says. "Let's have lunch."

"I am not going near Ag," I say.

"Steve won't be there," Charity says. "He's got detention."

"I know he has detention. I'm still not going there."

"You have to face it sometime, Angelyn."

"Come on," Jacey says. "We can watch the JV guys at lunch practice."

I look at her. "You mean, watch JT. You don't care if he sees you with me?"

"We have to hear your side, Angelyn. That's fair."

I tell her okay. But something still seems wrong.

We sit in the football bleachers, the school stretched before us. Across the athletic fields I see the outside corridor where Jeni and I stood this morning. The girls rummage for their food, Jacey next to me, Charity a row below.

"I shouldn't have said that to Jeni."

Charity squints at me. "Who?"

"You know who," I say.

"The bathroom girl," Jacey says. "I bet she's heard worse than that."

"Maybe," I say. "But not from me."

I stare out. From here, everything looks pretty.

We share what we have. Deli turkey and Kettle chips from Charity; celery sticks, string cheese, and cranberry bars from Jacey. Goldfish from me.

The JV boys trot out in practice clothes. JT notices me right off. He's staring up while the rest start their laps.

"You're in trouble," I tell Jacey.

She waves him on. "You and Steve will get back."

"No," I say.

"You have to," Charity says.

"What if I don't?"

"Then you're crazy," she says.

"Never mind now," Jacey says. "Tell us what happened."

I sort the details.

"We were at the reservoir, you know, parked, and Steve wanted to do more than I did."

Charity swirls her hands. "Go on, Angelyn!"

"We fought about it. And—he left me there."

Charity nods, like, *more, more.* I can't read Jacey.

"This *dog* was there," I say. "It turned out he dumped *her* too!"

Their expressions don't change.

"Steve came back, but he was a total ass about it. He said this stuff about you, Jacey." I nod to Charity. "And you too."

Charity touches her chest. *"Me?"*

Jacey is frowning. "You don't do everything with Steve?"

I blink. "Sometimes I do. I didn't want to then."

"You're playing him, Angelyn. JT wouldn't put up with it."

"But—we don't *have* to, right? They can't make us."

"Did Steve try to make you?" Jacey asks. "Really?"

"Well, no. You think it's okay he left me out there?"

"Steve told everyone he came right back," Charity says.

"He *told* that?" I curl away from them. "God, what else did he say?"

"He's a guy," Jacey says. "You pissed him off. You'll work it out."

"Steve was wrong." My voice is small. "I can be right."

"Just don't think you're better," Jacey says.

I look at her. "I didn't say that. I never did."

Charity grins.

"What's with you?" I ask, wishing I hadn't said a thing.

"Steve is coming." She says it like she's announcing Santa.

The lunch detention crew is sweeping across the field toward the track. A different teacher is with them today. Steve covers his territory like a wounded bear.

I ask the girls: "What do I do?"

Together they say: "Talk to him."

JT is flagging Steve and pointing to me. The detention teacher peels off to talk to the coach. Facing away, they laugh together.

I stand. "I'm not staying for this."

Steve shadows me along the track as I cross the length of the bleachers. I start down the steps, and he starts up them.

We meet somewhere in the middle.

Steve pushes his hair back with a muddy hand. "You hiding from me?"

I look at him until I can't. "What are you *saying* about me?"

"Huh?"

"This morning," I say, pushing past. "I heard all about it!"

"Angelyn!" He's on my heels.

I *run-stumble-jump* down the steps, grabbing the rail as I slip on one.

Steve blasts around me. Blocks me as I'm bent, breathless.

"What are you doing?" he asks.

I look up.

"You're wrecking me here!"

"You know we're over," I say.

"I don't know that," Steve says.

I straighten. "We're so over."

He waves an arm backward. "How do you think my folks took this?"

"Your detention? Mr. Rossi gave you that. I didn't."

"Rossi let you walk. I don't have a cute butt to shake, so here I am."

"Hey! We were late because of you, and that's why—"

"I was pissed at that," Steve says. "This morning, and you weren't there."

I wait. So does he.

"Is this you saying, *Sorry*?" I ask. "Because, some apology."

"It's the truth," he says. "I can't do better than that."

"Well, I'm not saying, *Oh, okay.* And, *It's all good.* No."

Steve turns up his hands. "No?"

"No." I say it softly. Direct. "Find another girl."

He teeters on the step. "What?"

"You heard me."

Steve is still as I pass him.

The detention crew watches in a knot on the track. The players too, heads turned, their drills in slow motion.

"You're still wrapped up about that dog, aren't you?" Steve calls.

Genius, I think.

"I'll get her for you, Angelyn. She's yours!"

He's not serious. "Too late!" I shout.

"For what?" Steve is at my shoulder.

I break from him. "For *us*."

The action on the field dies. The coach and teacher turn.

"Coslow!" the teacher calls. "Down, now."

The coach points at me. "This is off-limits for student lunch."

Hands at my elbows, Steve sets me to one side. "We'll talk later."

"We will not!" I call, watching as he trots down.

I follow at a distance. The detention crew is massed on the track. I step into them, and they part for me, barely. Someone smacks his lips. I flinch. The kid laughs, and the rest take it up. *Kiss-kiss* all around, from lips I'd never touch. I push through. From the field, a catcall—*oww*—and then another. The sound goes on, stretching like taffy, pulled from many mouths. The coach's whistle doesn't dent it.

Steve stands between the groups. Our eyes meet. He turns his back. Hands raised, he makes like he's conducting.

I pass him and all of them, my arm raised, a finger to the sky.

Against the sunbaked gym, I am seeing, hearing, and feeling it again.

71

Lunch is still on. Kids eat at picnic tables under the awning. The breezeway swarms with people all the way up to the street.

The girls come charging around the corner.

"The coach made us leave too." Charity's voice is high and breathy.

Jacey asks if I'm all right.

I peel myself from the wall. "Now do you believe me?"

"Believe what?" she says.

"Steve *really* wants you back," Charity says.

"Oh yeah." My throat catches. "Did you see what just happened?"

"I saw you guys talking."

"Talking. Yeah. Steve sold me out."

"Don't get dramatic," Jacey says.

"Angelyn is all about the drama," Charity says.

I point toward the field. "I did not make that up."

They look at me like the problem is mine.

"And what is this *crap* about listening to *my side*? If we're friends, there is no side. You're with me."

Jacey scratches her arm. Charity says, "You don't deserve him."

I look at her closely. "Oh my God. You think you have a chance."

She flushes pink. "No, it's just that Steve's a friend, and you're not being fair."

"Steve's a friend?" I say. "Then why'd he call you *skank*?"

"He did not!" Charity says.

I nod. "He did. Don't know *why*."

Her face shades to red. "Yeah, everyone knows you're the skank."

"Because I've actually done stuff with a guy."

Charity's mouth twists. "One guy? Try twenty. I hear anybody'll do."

I look at Jacey. "She can't say that to me."

"Charity, shut up," Jacey says. "Angelyn, forget it."

"I can't forget everything!"

Things get quiet around us.

"Girl fight," someone says.

"Walk away," Jacey says.

I nod. "I've got no reason to stay."

A hard look at Charity and I weave off through the watchers.

"Trash!" she calls after me. "Welfare witch!"

I swing around. Kids arc out of the way, clearing a path.

Charity's chest heaves. I look her over, head to toe.

"All that money and nothing to spend it on."

"You never should have been our friend." Her voice snaps like a loose wire.

"Who's *your* friend?" I ask. "Jacey's busy and Steve don't go for fugly."

Charity runs at me.

I throw my backpack down. She rumbles around it, banging into my chest, pinning my arms as I stagger backward.

A ring forms around us, kids yelling.

I piston my shoulders but Charity holds me like iron. We circle in a crazy dance.

"Stupid," I say, and she growls something back.

I lift a boot and bring it down on her sandal. She yowls and hops, and I work an arm free and smack her shoulder. Charity spins off.

"Enough?" I ask, shaking out my hand.

She runs at me again. I sidestep, grabbing a fistful of product-heavy hair. I yank it. Charity kicks at me, missing by inches as I work to stay behind.

"Stop now?" I ask, close to her ear.

She elbows my gut. I jerk back and my feet tangle with hers. We fall, landing hard, Charity on top. I stare at the circle above. Laughing faces—most of them. Yelling. Happy. Jacey, silent. Pale as milk.

Charity shifts and straddles me, and I shut my eyes, taking her sissy slaps like I deserve them. She's crying. I'm not. I hear her sobs and the roar above. It rises and falls, and rises and falls again.

Charity's weight lifts off. I breathe in, opening my eyes. Mr. Rossi is there. He sticks out a hand. I take it, and he pulls me to my feet.

"If it weren't for bad luck," he says, "would you have any luck at all?"

CHAPTER TWELVE

Mr. Rossi walks Charity and me to the vice principal's office.

"There," he says, pointing to a row of chairs outside Miss Bass's door.

Charity slumps into the closest one, sniffling.

I take the one at the end.

"Be ladies," he says, a smirk as he knocks and enters.

I shift to find a soft spot, my butt sore where I landed.

"Hate you," Charity slings over.

"You want more?" I ask. "Here?"

"No," she grumps.

Mr. Rossi walks out. "Miss Bass is calling your parents."

Both of us groan.

"You girls take it light," he says. It's dumb, but I smile at him.

Charity's mom shows first. I hear her in the hall asking people which way.

Charity sits up straight and sober.

I almost say, *Trade you.* I wouldn't. But I think it.

Mrs. Flint walks in, dressed like she's been to lunch somewhere.

"Charity." She stops. Hands on hips. "What happened?"

Charity opens her mouth. She looks at me. Shuts it.

"Never mind." Mrs. Flint pushes into the office.

"My daughter does not fight," she says, voice soaring.

"Better get in there," I say. Charity drags herself up.

"This is all about Angelyn Stark," Mrs. Flint says.

I lift my head, listening.

"I have told my daughter and *told* her to stay away from that girl."

Like Charity never does anything wrong.

Miss Bass tells Charity to shut the door.

As it closes: "Angelyn is pure trash," Mrs. Flint says. "Like her mother."

I stand. Gut aching. *Bitch.*

Mrs. Flint was a room mother. Every year. And Mom was—*Mom.*

The front-desk ladies are watching me.

When Mrs. Flint and Charity come out, I point.

"*She* jumped *me*. Truth."

Charity scoots like I've booted her. Mrs. Flint huffs after.

Miss Bass curls a finger.

The visitor's chair inside Miss Bass's office is a mile more comfortable.

"Mr. Rossi's story supports yours," she says at her desk.

Warmth spreads through me. "Really?"

Miss Bass nods. "He said Charity had the best of you."

Not sure I like that. "We fought, but it wasn't my idea."

"What did you fight about, Angelyn? It would help me to know."

"She's been on me all day. I can tell you that."

"Charity says you've been on her."

"She would."

"I'm inclined to believe you," Miss Bass says.

"You are?"

"I've heard good things, lately."

"Wow," I say softly to myself.

"That must be your mother," Miss Bass says.

Mom is outlined in the frosted glass, hand up to knock.

"Good things?" I say. "She won't believe them."

"You work for us, Sherry," Miss Bass says. "We appreciate that."

"Yes, ma'am," Mom says. "What exactly did Angelyn do?"

"Ask me," I say.

Mom says, "Quiet."

Miss Bass clears her throat.

"Angelyn had a physical fight with another girl. Charity Flint. A teacher intervened. It appeared to him that Angelyn was not the aggressor."

"Angelyn knows she's not supposed to fight at all."

"Yes," Miss Bass says. "But this is a change. This girl is one of her friends."

"It was probably over some boy," Mom says.

"Charity can't get close to any guy," I say.

"You'd be better off if *you* couldn't."

"Thanks, Mom."

"Dressed like that." She flips her hand to me. "Skin-tight everything."

We're dressed alike. T-shirts and jeans.

"On me it looks good," I say. Just above my breath.

Mom leans to Miss Bass. "She's got a history with boys. Scratch any problem with Angelyn and that's what you'll find."

"This fight was not about boys! Mostly not," I add.

"You see what I deal with?" Mom says.

Miss Bass taps a pen. "Mr. Rossi says Angelyn's work has improved."

"I thought I was here because of the fight," Mom says.

"Mr. Rossi is the teacher who brought the girls in."

Mom looks stumped. "Why would he say that?"

"Because it's true!" I almost shout it. "You've seen me do the work."

"Angelyn did bad," she says past me. "She needs to learn how to get along in this world."

"Well, yes," Miss Bass says, "but—"

"Can I hear Angelyn's punishment?"

"Two days' suspension," she says quietly.

Mom sits back. "Thank you. I'll bring her to work with me."

"There's no one to watch her at home, Sherry?"

"No."

"Can I go to the bathroom?" I ask, already standing.

Miss Bass nods. "Be sure you come back, Angelyn."

Mom says, "She damn well better."

I race-walk down the hallway, wanting—needing—OUT.

"Angelyn!" someone calls as I pass Attendance.

I duck back. Jeni and Nathan are mixed in with the line of kids for late passes. They cross to me, Nathan first.

"You okay?" he asks.

"We weren't sure where to go," Jeni says.

I stare at them. "Where to go for what?"

"We saw the fight," Nathan says.

"You saw the fight. So?"

"That other girl started it," he says.

"We want to tell—whoever—what we saw," Jeni says.

"That'd be Miss Bass," I say. "The vice principal. But why—"

"You shouldn't get in trouble, Angelyn," Nathan says.

"Stop it," I say.

The attendance clerk cranes around. "You three! Get in line or get out."

Nathan and Jeni follow me into the hall.

"So, you don't want us to say anything?" Jeni asks.

I look toward the exit. "I don't know. You can. Whatever!"

Then it hits me.

"My *mom's* in with Miss Bass. Nathan, did she see you?"

He looks back blankly. "Your mom? I didn't see her."

I take a pinch of his moldy army jacket. "Let's go."

Leaving the building is like coming up for air. I stop, and stumble when Nathan bumps me. I pull him across the courtyard to a windowless wall.

Nathan is grinning at me. *Grinning.* I drop his sleeve.

"Don't get any ideas," I say.

"You've got dirt on your face." He touches his cheek. "Here."

I rub the spot with the heel of my hand. "Stop *noticing*, all right?"

"Jeni and me were coming down the hill when we saw you."

"Whose idea was it to go to the office?" I ask.

"Mine." Nathan sounds proud.

"I don't need your help, or hers. I've got things under control."

"Your mom isn't blaming you?"

"Yeah, she is. She'd do it worse if *you* showed up."

"That's not fair," he says. "She's not fair to both of us."

"Nathan, the best thing you can do for me is *leave me be*."

I whip away from him.

"I was right to tell," he says. Not loud but it goes through me.

I walk back. "You were right to tell what?"

Nathan blinks. "About your stepdad touching you."

I fall away. "Don't say that here. That lie."

"It's not a lie."

I want to scream at him. *Scream.* I look around. No one.

"You wrecked us with it. My whole family. Done."

"Grandma said I was right to tell."

"You lied to *her* too. Yes, you did!"

Nathan shifts his weight. "Naw."

With a look I pin him to the wall.

"You see one thing—*one thing*—you don't understand, and that's it. Time to—tear down the walls. Break everything. Did it make you feel special?"

From a distance Mom shouts my name. I catch my breath.

"I've got to go." I jab a finger at him. "Do not follow me!"

"I didn't see it once," Nathan says.

"What's that?"

"Your stepdad and you. I didn't see it once. I saw it a bunch."

"Freak." I whisper it.

"I *told* once."

"You were wrong." The words come out cracked.

"I was right. I never lied, Angelyn. You did, about him."

"Shut up."

Nathan searches me. "I hear he's still around. How can that be?"

Mom calls again, closer.

"Go," I tell him.

"She ought to know," Nathan says.

"*Go.*"

"Did you ever tell her? I mean, *you* telling her?"

I look toward the office. "Go, all right?"

"You should tell her, Angelyn."

I grit it out: "Please."

"Tell her the truth."

"Then I'll go." I push myself forward.

Mom comes around the building.

Each of us stops short.

"Well," she says. Red-faced. Sharp-voiced.

"Mom." I'm heavy, waiting.

"You know Miss Bass meant for you to use the bathroom in the building."

"Oh." I nod after. "Sure." I stare at Mom. Her eyes stay on me.

"We're not done in there, Angelyn. Now, come on."

Following, I look back. Nathan is gone.

CHAPTER THIRTEEN

Monday after the suspension, I start up the steps of the Humanities Building.

Jeni looks up from her book. "Angelyn?"

"Yep. I'm back."

"I didn't figure you'd be back here," she says.

"I've got nowhere else to go," I say. "For I don't know how long."

I settle cross-legged against the wall outside my English classroom.

"Did that girl get the same time off as you?" Jeni asks.

"We both got two days. That's what you get here when you fight unless it's real serious."

"Oh." Jeni rests her head on bent knee.

"I know you talked to Miss Bass about me."

"I guess it didn't help."

"My mom heard. One more person saying it wasn't all me."

Jeni nods. "Nathan said she's really rough on you."

"Hey! Don't talk about Nathan. Don't talk about my mother."

"Sorry."

"Why'd she get to keep the friends?" Jeni asks after a while.

"Charity? It's complicated."

"The whole *friend* thing is," she says.

"Why did you talk to Miss Bass?" I ask.

Jeni looks at me. Shrugs.

"I know it was *his* idea," I say.

"Nathan says you're always in trouble."

I rise. "What?"

"Angelyn!" Jeni stands too. "I don't want to fight with you."

"Who's fighting?" I ask, my back to the wall.

"I think I shouldn't wait here."

"Don't leave. I just don't get it. Why'd you speak for me?"

"You mean, after what you said about me in class?"

We both look at her shoes. They're the same shoes.

"I shouldn't have said it. We don't have much either."

"Okay, Angelyn," Jeni says. "Okay."

"It isn't. Unless you are way different than I am."

"Well . . . ," she says.

I cross to the steps. "Sit down. We can sit."

Jeni does. I do. She keeps an eye on me.

"I can't keep up with my friends," I say. "On clothes. Most all of my stuff is discount. They know it."

"Do they get on you for that?" Jeni asks.

"Charity will. I'll tell you something. I got to be friends with them in fourth grade because we were always the ones getting called out by the teacher. It was always *us* on the punishment bench at lunch recess, you know? I never thought Jacey and Charity were any different from me. But the day before

Christmas break, they came to school with big paper sacks. They gave them to me."

Jeni's wincing. "Clothes inside?"

"Yeah. *Their* clothes. Their moms were working on a Christmas clothing drive, and they got the idea. Like I would wear their stuff. Like I *could*. Charity's fatter than me and Jacey's thinner."

"So, what did you do?"

"I got mad. I kicked the bags around. Everyone saw. Everybody knew."

"And those girls are still your friends?"

"We got to be, again. I had to hang with someone."

"I got suspended a few times in junior high," Jeni says. "Always because some *friend* talked me into doing something stupid. Half the time they'd get off."

I listen. "Never you?"

"I'm a bad liar. A terrible liar. I'd say it all. About myself."

"I never tell," I say, "but I still get in trouble. Once Jacey and me got into trouble together. Mom grounded me and I had to do extra chores and stuff. All that happened to Jacey was I couldn't come to her house anymore. Charity's mother got in on it and I couldn't go *there* either. I used to be tight with Jacey, and Charity ran after us. It was never like that again."

"This is my seventh school," Jeni says. "No, eighth. It's my eighth. And, it's always been—the smart kids don't want me because I don't look or dress like them. The poor kids don't like me because I don't talk like them. I used to try to fit in. Now I know I don't need friends."

"I don't need friends either," I say.

She looks at me. "I think ahead, Angelyn."

I shift. "Ahead to what?"

"My life. When I'm living how I want. I can't wait."

"Oh," I say.

"I'm going to be a nurse," Jeni says. Like she's sure of it. "How about you?"

I reach for something. "The Coast Guard?"

"You're going to join the Coast Guard? That's cool."

It does sound cool. All I have to do is find out what it means.

Voices at the corner. Ms. Hinsley, my English teacher, comes around.

"Angelyn Stark is off suspension," she says.

You can hear the *ick* in her voice.

Mr. Rossi is next, cradling a steaming mug.

"Don't let her fool you," he says. "Angelyn Stark is one smart girl."

"I am not opening the classroom this early, Angelyn," Ms. Hinsley says.

I slouch on the steps. "Didn't ask you to."

"Yeah, we've got some donuts to walk off," Mr. Rossi says.

Ms. Hinsley *clickety-clack*s by.

After her, Mr. Rossi winks.

I'm laughing.

"What do you think of him?" I ask.

"He gave me detention first day," Jeni says.

I watch them go. "I think he's pretty great."

■ ■ ■

Charity's foot is parked on my desk when I walk into World
Cultures.

"Move it," I say, staring down the aisle.

She points to Jeni at the window. "Sit *there*. We don't want
you."

One row over, Jacey is zombielike. No help.

I start to argue, then—*why not?*

"Mr. Rossi?"

He lowers his newspaper. "Yes, Angelyn?"

"Can I change seats?"

Mr. Rossi takes me in. Charity with her foot on my desk. Jeni
by the window.

"You bet," he says.

At lunch I climb with Jeni toward town.

"You're all right with us being partners?" she says.

"I don't mind, but I didn't get everything he was saying."

Jeni talks about the project Mr. Rossi assigned:

Choose a country; research an issue that affects it.

"Those girls were pissed not to have you in their group," she
says.

"They were not. We'd all three fail together."

Her words lift me.

The sidewalk rises steeply. Jeni falls behind. I wait and walk
slower. It's strange to walk with someone new. Two instead
of three.

"We could work on the report before school," she says. "In the library."

"The library?" I make a face. "I guess I don't have anywhere else to be then."

"It's got to be there," Jeni says. "We can't work where I'm living."

"We sure can't work at my place."

Near the top of the hill a truck pulls even with us. Stays even. I know the sound.

"Whatever you hear," I say, "*don't* hear it. *Don't* look."

Jeni says, "What?"

"The truck," I say. "It's my boyfriend. He's following us."

As we step into the crosswalk: "I know that ass!" some guy calls.

Not even Steve's voice.

Into town we're trailed by the *squeal-stop* of Steve's brakes.

"Why is he following?" Jeni sounds scared.

I toss my hair. "They're not after you."

"Angelyn. Angelyn!" That same guy's voice that I can't place.

We pass a parking garage. City Hall. A Mexican restaurant.

Then: "ANGELYN!" My name in chorus. Finally, I look.

Steve is rolling next to us. Three hangers-on from our group are in the back of the truck. Young kids. The ones without girls. My choir.

In the cab with him, a friend from last year. Kal somebody. He's graduated.

"It takes five of you to make *one*," I shout.

Kal slings an arm out the window. "How 'bout we all make *you*?"

I look to Steve. "You let him say that?"

Steve shoots me the finger. Wiggles it.

Jeni tugs at me. "Angelyn—"

I whirl on her. "Hands off."

She reels away. Hurt eyes.

Two lawyer types look us over, passing. We're close to Courthouse Park.

"Come on, let's go," I say.

The boys yell after us. Steve honks.

"They're stopped in traffic," Jeni says.

In the park I take a bench that faces the street.

"Leave if you want," I say.

Jeni sinks onto the bench.

I swallow. "When they come, pretend—"

"Like we don't care," she says. "No matter what."

I look at her. "Yes."

Steve is heavy on the bumper of the car in front. The boys in the back are pointing to the park like they've discovered land.

"What's he need all those guys for?" I wonder out loud.

"I've got some gummy worms," Jeni says.

"And you're telling me because?"

"We could look busy eating them."

"Dig them out," I say.

She pulls a bag from her purse, and we each take some.

"These are horrible," I say, chewing. Like globs of stale Jell-O.

She folds a leg under. I stretch my arms along the bench back.

"Lesbos!" the boys shout as the truck inches to the park.

I blow them a kiss across the empty sidewalk.

Jeni's hand trembles as she passes me the bag.

"Look at that slut," Kal calls as the truck pulls parallel to us.

"Hey!" I say, standing. "Steve! Shut him up. Talk for yourself."

Steve is slumped, shades on. The car he's tailing surges ahead.

"Go!" I call as traffic builds behind him.

He throws down his shades, puts the truck in park, and jumps out.

Jeni chokes my name.

"It's okay," I tell her. Thinking: *Is it?*

Steve stomps around the truck and onto the sidewalk. People are honking.

"What?" I call. "What?" when he's closer.

"We are on our way to Taco Bell," he says. Steaming.

I tilt my chin. "And you're driving the bus? The *short* bus."

"It ain't about you, Angelyn! That's what I'm saying."

"Then tell them to stop."

Steve thumbs back. "I don't tell them what to say! They say it."

"Like on the field?" My breath hitches. "They don't hear it first from you?"

He frowns. "Why are you doing this?"

"Doing what?"

"Holding out," Steve says.

We eye each other.

"I'm not your bitch," I say.

"Since when?" Steve asks.

"Since right this second." I fire the words at him.

"Angelyn, damn."

I point. "I'd be looking at *that*."

Kal is jerking the truck down Main, the boys in back bouncing like beans.

"Shit." Steve takes off running.

I sit back on the bench.

"That was great," Jeni says.

"That was acting," I say, working my cold fingers.

"He never saw me."

"Steve can be single-minded."

"My mom meets guys off the Internet," Jeni says.

"What?"

"That's how she got with Nathan's dad. That's why we're in this town."

"Okay, why are you telling me?"

"Just thinking out loud, Angelyn."

"Your mom trolls the Net for sex buddies and I need to know."

Jeni laughs. "*Romance*, she calls it."

I'm not sure how to take her. "Well, I'm not like that."

"I'm not either." Deadly serious now. "I won't be. Not ever."

A clump of regular people goes by, coffee and cigarettes in hand. A jury, I decide, on break from one of the courts.

"My mother hates me," I say.

"Why?" Jeni asks.

"She just does. Forget it." My face is hot.

"Okay." She checks her watch. "Maybe we should go."

We leave the park.

"You think we'll get back to school before those guys do?" Jeni asks.

"Yep." Taco Bell is on the far end of town.

"Angelyn, I feel like I said the wrong thing, but I don't know what it is."

I exhale. "No, I did. There's no point in talking about it."

"My mom is kind of—out there," Jeni says.

"But do you get along with her?" I ask.

"She's not a grown-up. Sometimes I have to think for both of us. But, yeah, we get along."

"Any of her Net friends ever go for you?"

"They get her, not me." Jeni is calm. "We are real clear on that one."

I scuff along the sidewalk.

We pass lawyers' offices done up in cozy brick-red. Superior Court, its sparkling glass door stuck between yellow brick walls.

I point. "They hear custody cases in there. My mom used to say I'd best watch myself, or that's where we'd all wind up."

Jeni is looking at me. "You mean, like, your dad would try to get you?"

Rage starts through me. It dies. "No. Like the state would try to get me."

"Oh." Her voice is careful.

"Nathan told you all about me, I bet."

"He said some things. Not in a bad way. He likes you, for sure."

"It's all bad. And Nathan's a punk."

We're quiet, climbing. We stop at the intersection.

"I think about what comes next," Jeni says. "What *I* can do. I already know I won't be like my mom, waiting on some guy. I'm going to make my own life."

She's shiny-faced, breathless, her hair escaping from its knot.

"I don't see ahead," I say. "For me it's all about getting by."

"I *have* to see ahead. My life would suck too much if I didn't."

"I can't be more than what I am." I test the words.

Jeni asks, "Why not?"

CHAPTER FOURTEEN

I look at her. At him. At dinner. It's always the same. Mom talks and Danny says nothing. She hardly looks at him, and he only looks at his food. What keeps them together—I wonder—*still*.

I hate how the kitchen shrinks when all of us are in it.

"Someone pass the juice?" I say.

The container is closest to Danny.

He keeps his eyes down. I can *feel* him wanting to reach.

"Lazy," Mom says. "Get it yourself."

With a swipe of my arm, I grab the bottle. Danny flinches.

"Sorry." I watch his bowed head.

Mom talks more. Something about her boss. Something about the job.

I push my chair back. "Can I be excused?"

"So rude," Mom says.

"What?" I say. "I'm done. I've got homework."

"I tell you my news and you ask to leave?"

Her eyes have me pinned. Dark eyes, almost black. Like mine.

I look back, lost.

"Are you happy for me?" Mom asks.

"Yeah." No clue. "Congratulations."

"Thanks. What for?"

I'm squirming. "I didn't hear your news. Sorry."

Danny glugs water.

"Angelyn, you didn't *listen*. I hate liars."

My throat clutches like her hand's around it.

"I'll listen now."

Mom picks up a breadstick. Swabs it in sauce.

"Tell me, all right?"

"You'll have to wait until the weekend," she says, chewing around the words.

95

"The weekend?" It's Thursday. "What's happening then?"

"We are going shopping," Mom says. "And out to lunch."

It's not my birthday. Not Christmas. "Shopping for what?"

"I want to buy you a treat."

Now I'm staring. "Why? I mean, thanks—but why?"

"You'll find out." Mom breaks out smiling. "I don't mind telling it twice."

With shoulders and attitude, Mom clears a path through the packed aisles of Rowdy's shoe department, grabbing boxes off shelves, passing them to me.

"Choose one," she says when we have three.

In an empty corner I line the boxes on a bench.

"How'd you know my size?" I ask, stepping out of my past-it summer sandals.

"We both take nine."

I lift the lid off the first box. Running shoes. Pretty nice ones. They fit fine. Look good. I have a pair like them at home.

The second box holds brown clogs with fake-fur yellow trim. I turn one over. "They look like bear paws."

"Winter's coming," Mom says. "Try them out."

I clump around, uglier with every step.

"Those are really cute," she says.

"They kill my feet," I say. A lie. I'd never wear them.

Mom points to the last box.

Ballet flats. I slip them on and slide along the floor. The fabric pinches the sides of my feet and feels like nothing underneath.

I take them off. "Can I look around?"

Her mouth turns down. "I don't know what you think you want."

I'm backstepping. "Five minutes. *Less* than five."

Mom just looks at me. But she doesn't say no.

Families from toddlers to grandmas are picking through shoes, hopping in, testing walks. I weave through, scanning displays.

Then I see them. *The shoes.* Stiletto-heeled Mary Janes, ribbon straps, *red*, standing out like jewels in a sea of black and brown.

I find my size. Cradling the box, I take it to Mom.

"You're kidding," she says when I lift the shoes out.

They fit like custom-made. Feel great walking. In the step-stool mirror I check front, side, and back. My legs are long, strong, endless.

I can't stop smiling. "These are the ones I want."

"What would you use them for, Angelyn?"

"Dances? You said it was a treat."

"You want to look pretty for *all the boys*," Mom says. "Right?"

My stomach dips. "No. Not really. I mean, I like the shoes for me."

"Why?"

I stick a foot out, looking. "It's not complicated. They're pretty. *They* are."

Mom checks the box. "Ninety dollars."

"Ninety." I sit on the bench. "I didn't see that."

"Ninety dollars." Her voice is hard.

I pull the shoes off. "Okay, Mom."

Taking one, she fingers a ribbon. "I used to want things like this. I never got them."

"You didn't?" I say, watching her.

"We were too poor." Mom is somewhere else. "I've brought you a long way, Angelyn."

I shrug. And sneak a look at the shoes before they go back in the box.

"Why *do* you want them?" Mom's voice is intense.

Surprised, I raise my eyes. "They make me happy." My face flushes, but it's true.

She boxes the shoes and walks them past me.

We stand at the end of a very long line. Mom's back is to me, her arm curved around the box.

"Thanks?" I say.

I see the price on the box end—$90.

"Really, Mom. I can't believe it. I mean it—thanks."

"All right," she says.

We shuffle forward with the line.

"You can borrow them sometimes," I say.

Mom turns. "What?"

I smile a little. "We are the same size."

She looks me up and down. "I wouldn't wear these outside the bedroom."

My smile sticks. "Mom—that's disgusting."

"Yes, it is."

She's mad. The woman in front of her is turned and staring.

I reach for the box. "I'll take the running shoes instead."

Mom swings away. "No, ma'am. You made your choice."

In a diner across the parking lot, Mom tells me her news. Her eyes shine. It's like the store never happened.

"It's a great opportunity," she says. "They *asked* me to apply."

I sip my Diet Coke, the bulky shoe box pressed to my thigh.

Mom pulls back. "You can't say you didn't hear me this time."

"I'm just not that excited about you becoming a bus driver."

"Angelyn, it's twice the money. Overtime hours. Better insurance."

"That's why the shoes," I say.

Mom's face falls, like a little kid's. Then it gets mean. "Most girls would be happy to shop with their mothers. Most girls would be glad for a new pair of shoes."

The waitress steps up with our food. Burgers and fries. We eat in quiet.

"This is going to change our lives," Mom says, wiping her lips. "You don't see that now, Angelyn, but you will."

I'm thinking. "You'll be out of the house more. Right? With overtime and things."

She looks at me quickly. "Yes. Why? You've got something planned?"

"No. I don't. Is Danny all jazzed about this?"

Mom doesn't answer right off. "Sure he is. *He's* excited for me."

"How is that going to be—" I lose my nerve.

"How is *what* going to be?"

"Nothing," I say. "Wow, more money coming in. Danny won't even have to *pretend* to work."

"You're missing the point," Mom says. "And I don't like your tone."

The hostess leads a group to the booth across from ours. A tourist family by their look, right out of L.L.Bean. Blond dad, blond mom, two kids, a boy and toddler girl.

They've hardly sat before the girl turns up her arms to the man. He sweeps her into his lap, and she settles against his chest like it's a pillow.

The girl waves, smiling—"Hi!"—at me.

I look away. And catch Mom's eye. She was watching too.

"My real dad," I say. "Did he— It's hard to ask, but—"

"Your *real* dad. He is long gone."

A deep voice. My name the way he said it: *Angie-lyn.*

"I don't remember much. But—did he ever care?"

Mom lifts her chin. "Not how Danny cares."

"Oh."

"Junk jobs. *Part-time* junk jobs. That's all I could get until Danny got me on at the high school."

"And then they let him go," I say.

"He was injured on the job!"

"*Whatever* happened."

"Danny fell off a ladder. He settled with the district, and that's how he got his work truck. You know all that."

"Okay, Mom."

"They wouldn't have given him a settlement if he'd done something wrong."

"Mom. Okay."

"Danny helped me. He helped *us* when no one else wanted to know. I don't forget that."

What do you remember? I want to ask.

Instead: "So, it's all right with you that we'll be spending more time together? Danny and me. While you're driving the bus."

And then I can't look at her.

"Angelyn." Mom is hushed. "What is your problem?"

I study my plate.

"My news. And you make it about you."

"Sorry." I hate saying it.

"Don't be like this on our trip. I want to make it fun."

I look up. "What trip?"

"I don't have the job yet," Mom says. "I've got training in Sacramento next weekend, and a couple of weekends after that. You're coming with."

"I am?"

"I'll get a motel with a pool, so you can swim. And good TV. Maybe room service. The district is paying."

"Why do I have to go?"

"Come on." Mom fake-laughs. "Pretend you're a normal kid."

"I've got homework." My voice is heavy. "Every weekend."

"Bring your books! I'll be out all day, both days, training."

"Mom, I don't want to go."

"You're going." Steely.

She signals for the check.

"I know why," I say quietly.

Mom zooms in on me. "You know what?"

"A trip with you is not about *fun*."

"Thanks!"

"It's about Danny," I say. "And me. You don't want to leave us alone."

"Wrong," she says.

"If you take the job, we'll *be* alone. What happens then?"

Mom blinks through mascara.

"Trust us now or trust us later. You have to do it sometime."

Her lashes catch. "You ruin everything."

Mom slides from the booth, grabbing at her purse. Throws

money at the table and walks out fast. The diner doors swing after her.

I watch it all, numb.

The waitress is at the table. "Trouble?"

I point to the money.

She scoops it and leaves.

I take the shoes from the box. Pull them on.

As I stand, a little voice calls, "Pretty!" The L.L.Bean mom says, *"Hush."*

I think I thank the girl.

Mom is in the truck.

I climb in. "I'm surprised you waited."

"You're my responsibility, Angelyn."

I stare at my beautiful feet. "Thanks for the shoes."

"Where are the old ones?"

"Oh!" I look over. "In the diner. I could go back—"

"No." She starts the truck.

We're quiet all the way home.

Into the carport, Mom lets the motor idle.

"You're going to Sacramento."

"No," I say. "You can't force me into the truck."

"You're going!" she says. "And I won't be nice about it."

"What would happen if I stayed with him?"

Mom stares at me.

"Nothing. Right?"

"Right," she says.

"I spent my suspension with you—two days copying and stapling. I couldn't stay at home. Mom, why couldn't I?"

"You're my kid, not Danny's. He wouldn't watch you like I would."

Fingers and thumbs, I rub my face.

"Why are you talking this way?" Mom's words poke at me. "Why are you doing it now?"

"Why did you talk that way in the store?" I ask, and hold my breath.

"Angelyn—what? I bought the shoes you wanted. I spent that money on you."

I drop my hands and study them. "Yeah, Mom."

"Look at me." I do. "I am getting this job. And you are not going to distract me."

"Oh, sorry for *distracting* you," I say in a hot rush.

"I won't let you," Mom says.

CHAPTER FIFTEEN

Jeni takes another note. Books are stacked between us. I look out on our class scattered through the library.

"Wish I'd known he'd bring us here," I say. "We wouldn't have had to come before school."

"We need the time," Jeni says. "All of it. We're getting an A on this."

"*You* are," I say, eyeing my closed notebook. "I can't concentrate."

Jacey and Charity sit a few tables away, shoulder to shoulder, whispering.

"They're talking about me," I say.

"Maybe not," Jeni says.

Charity turns. Makes a face. Says something to Jacey. They laugh.

I look at Jeni. "No, huh?"

"Well . . ." She bites her lip. "*Here.*" Pushing some copied pages my way.

I flick at them. "What are these?"

"It's an article about Australia and immigration."

"Sounds hot."

"This one's about *early* immigration," Jeni says.

I laugh. "Oh, *early* immigration."

"Angelyn, if you read it, you'll like it. Seriously. Some of the first ones to come over were prisoners. England sent them. People they didn't want."

"Okay," I say. Not convinced.

"It's about second chances." Jeni is intense.

I start to page through. "I will look."

Sound rises and falls through the room. Mr. Rossi stands at the counter with the librarian and the career counselor.

"Why would somebody like him be a teacher, you think?"

Jeni looks up. "Mr. Rossi? Why not? He's like any of them."

"I don't think so," I say.

She points to the article. "Take notes."

I flip and scan like I know what I'm doing.

Somebody's cell goes off—loud. *BAA PAA PAA PAA.* Game-show ringtone.

People laugh and look around.

Mr. Rossi's grabbing at a pants pocket. It's his phone.

He takes it out. Drops it. "Shit!" he says, and everyone gets quiet.

Stooping, Mr. Rossi punches at the phone. "Wait," he says into it.

He walks it outside.

"Weird," Jeni says. Kids are buzzing.

Through the glassed panels, I see Mr. Rossi pacing, talking, listening.

"Something's wrong," I say.

"That's his business." She's back to her book.

I take up the article. Details catch me. I start over from page one.

"That *is* cool," I say when I'm done. "About the prisoners."

Jeni checks me. "Yeah?"

"There's a line here." I find it. "How in Australia they could write their own endings."

She nods. "Beginnings too. It didn't matter what they came from."

"What they'd done," I say.

"What anyone did to them," Jeni says.

I'm writing. "I guess I could do this part of the report."

She smiles. "That's great, Angelyn."

"Twue wuv!" Charity's voice carries. We look at her.

"You're the one close enough to chew Jacey's gum," I say.

They burn carpet scraping chairs from each other.

Guys at the table between us laugh.

Jacey pouts. "God, Angelyn."

I point to Charity. "Tell her."

Jacey runs her eyes over Jeni. "So, this is your new best friend?"

"My partner for this project. Good luck with yours."

"What are you trying to prove, Angelyn? Sticking with her."

"What are you doing, Jacey, standing by whatever *she* does?"

Jacey checks Charity. I'm pissed at myself for saying that much.

I jerk my head to Jeni. "You guys chose her for me. Charity did."

"But you're not even trying to get back," Jacey says. "Not with us. Not with Steve."

"Why don't you draw me a map?" I say.

"Come on," Charity says, standing. "Let's leave them be happy together."

"You're pathetic," I say. "Both of you are."

Jacey and Charity gather their things.

"Do you want to be with them?" Jeni asks.

I look at her. "Not today. Does it sound like I do?"

"A little." She's sunk in the chair, the book to her face.

"Don't you be pissed at me, Jeni. Not you too."

"I'm not pissed," she says. "I don't care. I only want to work."

"Forget what I said about Charity choosing you."

"Why? It's only true. But it doesn't matter."

"It *doesn't*," I say. "I never think about it."

"Sure you do, or you wouldn't have said it."

"Hey—"

"Angelyn, it's okay. We're not friends. Partners, right?"

Jacey and Charity are at the magazine wall, talking.

"We really were friends," I say. "Jacey and me. She just dropped it."

Jeni says, "Forget her."

"You're right." I stare at the article I've read, trying to feel it again.

"You know, we're kind of on a roll. Want to work in here at lunch?"

"The library at lunch? You're killing me with this stuff. But, yeah. Okay."

"Good," Jeni says.

The doors to the library fly in. Nathan runs through.

"What's *he* doing?" I ask.

He stops in front, checking the room.

Jeni stands. "Nathan!"

His face clears. She scoops her backpack.

"What's going on?" I say.

"Trouble," Jeni says, her lips in a line.

"Nice *friends*, Angelyn," Charity calls as Jeni crosses.

Mr. Rossi pushes into the library as Nathan and Jeni dash out.

"Hey!" he says, sidestepping. "Stop."

They're gone.

"What just happened?" Mr. Rossi asks the room.

No one answers.

Jeni doesn't show at lunch. I sit at the fountain outside the library, cursing Nathan and his drama. All around me, kids are yelling, laughing, *eating*. I've got nothing.

The door to the teachers' lounge swings open in the breezeway between the library and Administration. Mr. Rossi steps through, a paper sack in hand.

His expression lightens as I walk up to him. "Angelyn."

"Mr. Rossi." I'm smiling. "Can I ask you something? Kind of crazy."

"After today— Sure, what is it?"

"Can I bum some food off you? I forgot to bring lunch."

"You want to have lunch with me?" he says.

"There's no one else," I say. Then: "Wait! I didn't mean—"

Mr. Rossi has this sarcastic grin. "I am one popular guy."

I lift my shoulders. "I didn't ask right. But, can we?"

"You know," he says, "you bet."

Mr. Rossi lines his lunch along his desk. "Such as it is."

A ham sandwich. Grapes. Something in a plastic container.

He points to it. "Pasta salad. Take your pick."

I sit opposite him. "The grapes, I guess."

Mr. Rossi raises a finger. "And half the sandwich."

"Okay." I lean for the food.

He pops the lid off the salad. And reels backward.

"Can something go bad between this morning and now?"

I'm covering my nose. "Definitely, yes." Laughing.

He seals the salad and dumps it. "Welcome to my day."

"Aw. Well, mine's not any better."

Mr. Rossi leans back, arms behind his head. "Tell me something good, Angelyn."

I eat a grape. "I'd have to make it up."

"The dog is working out. You ought to like that."

"She is? That's great. Your son is lucky to have Dolly."

"Yes," he says. "So, why are you on your own today?"

I poke at the ham sandwich. "Short on friends, I guess."

"They let you down?"

"Everyone does that."

He looks sad. "You're young to know that for a fact."

"Some people are okay. You are."

Mr. Rossi's chair creaks. "Nice of you to say so."

"Thanks for letting me eat here."

He picks up his sandwich half. "This ham doesn't look too good."

I don't think it does either, but I keep quiet.

"Hey, Angelyn. Want to see a picture of my son?"

"Sure! I'd like that."

Nodding me over, Mr. Rossi pulls out his wallet.

At his shoulder I lean to the picture—a blond, green-eyed toddler smiling on a bale of hay.

"Halloween last year," Mr. Rossi says. "We went to a pumpkin patch."

"He's cute," I say. "He looks happy."

Mr. Rossi stares at the picture. "Camden is my world."

I try to imagine Mom—anyone—saying that about me.

"I'm not such a bad guy if this kid loves me."

"Mr. Rossi." I'm surprised. "You're not a bad guy at all."

His head dips.

"Mr. Rossi?"

He breathes in hard.

I'm scared. "Camden is all right, isn't he?"

A hand up, he nods.

"Well—what's wrong?"

He makes a sound. Mr. Rossi is crying.

"Oh!" My hand hovers at his shoulder. "Oh, don't."

"She took him, Angelyn. My wife. Took Camden and left me."

"She did?" I hurt all through for him. "That sucks so bad."

"It does. I don't know what to do."

"You'll get him back. I know you will, because you care."

He wipes his eyes. "I can't do this. Not here. Can't let anyone see."

Both of us look to the door.

"If anybody gets on you, Mr. Rossi, I'll kick their butt."

Silence. Then he laughs.

"You are really something, Angelyn."

"Something good?" I ask, looking down at him. *Don't laugh at me.*

"Yes," he says. "One tough little angel."

CHAPTER SIXTEEN

Next morning, Mom is all snappy business.

"Up," she says in the doorway. "I want to be on the road."

I blink from the bed. *Sacramento*. "I am not going."

"I've reconsidered that. Now hurry. I'll drop you at school."

I stumble around the room picking what's closest to wear. Dark T from yesterday. Jeans from yesterday, puddled on the floor. I slide on flip-flops.

Mom yells for me to come.

I circle for my backpack. It's under the bed, and I drop to grab it. Behind the backpack, the *shoes* peek out like hopeful dogs, dusty, waiting. I don't want them now.

The kitchen door slams.

I run for it—*slap-slap*—not caring if the noise wakes Danny. *Danny.* Mom never *reconsiders* anything. I check their room. Empty.

He's in the truck with her. Mom is at the wheel.

I step to them through wet grass. "What's going on?"

"Danny's coming with me to Sacramento," Mom says.

"*He* is? Why?"

She starts the truck. "Get in, Angelyn."

Danny's like a lump. Like some robot she steers.

"I am not sitting three in a seat with you and him."

"That's right," Mom says. "You're not."

The cab is stuffed with their gear.

"You don't mean I should ride in the back."

Her lips quirk. "Yeah. I do."

The bed is unlined. Cold metal speckled with yard waste.

I cross my arms. "That's not fair."

"Life isn't," Mom says.

Danny looks across. "That's right."

I look back. "*You're* pissed at me? Why? This is all her."

His face purples.

"Don't talk to him," Mom says.

I step away. "I'll take the bus."

"No, you'll climb in."

"And if I don't?"

"Your choice," Mom says. "I drop you at school or report you truant."

The miles go by faster on the outside. I sit against a wheel well, backpack between my knees. Inside, Mom talks to Danny, gesturing one-handed. About me I am sure. The wind tugs my hair and flips it in my eyes. I shut them for protection and against the sight of the two in front.

In town I can hear them—my name mentioned—and I press hands to ears. My hair feels rough. I try to work fingers through and can't.

I stick an arm in the backpack, feeling for a comb. Nothing.

"Shit," I say, and brush back tears.

"Nice hair!" some kid calls from a sidewalk near the high school.

Mom drives past the auditorium. I see Steve's group ahead by Ag.

Pride aside, I scrape the cab window open.

"Mom, turn back. I'm fighting with those kids."

She drives on. Danny looks between us.

I crouch at the window. *"Please."*

Mom says, "Don't ask me for anything."

"Oh." I sit on my heels. She steps on it, and I fall. Mom swerves and stops the truck. I roll up on hands and knees. We're parallel to the Ag building. Steve, JT, Jacey, Charity, and the others line the sidewalk.

"I hate you," I say. Quiet.

Mom says, "Get out."

I swing a leg over the side. Cold in T and flip-flops, I drop to the ground.

"Hate you!" I scream it, reaching for the backpack.

She jerks the truck forward. My fingers scrape the strap. Mom swings into a U-turn, speeding off with Danny like they're a pair of kids.

I'm left there, nothing in my hands. Shivering. So embarrassed.

Something hits me on the butt. Something light, thrown hard. It skids into the street. A purple plastic comb.

"Fix your hair, bitch," Charity says.

I stare at the comb. Afraid to turn.

"That's not right." Steve is talking. "Angelyn, are you okay?"

"Totally." I try for sarcastic. It comes out strangled.

"She looks homeless." Charity again.

"Shut up." It's Jacey.

I turn.

Everyone is staring. Charity is closest, off the sidewalk.

I look at Jacey. "Got something I can use?" I mime brushing my hair.

She digs in her purse. "Hang on."

"You don't have to help her," Charity says.

Jacey pulls out a brush.

Steve sticks his hand out. "Give it here."

Pulling a face, she hands it to him.

With a tiny shrug, I start to leave.

Steve says, "Don't run."

I check traffic. "Who's running?"

"I'll brush your hair." He's closer.

I whirl around. "No way."

"Come on, Angelyn," Steve says.

"With them watching?"

"Yeah."

"Forget it."

He comes the rest of the way. "Who else is going to do it?"

I look up at him. "No games."

Steve grins. "I want to be your hair boy."

It's hard not to grin back. "My *what*?"

"I'll show you."

I let him turn me.

Steve sets the brush at my hairline. He pulls it back. I flinch with a snag. He stops himself and starts again, slowly. By the time he's done a section—the brush pulled clean to my shoulder blade—I'm breathless.

"Guess it was bad," I say, touching what Steve's made smooth.

"Like Mrs. Frankenstein," he says.

"Well, keep going."

He does. The bristles tickle as the knots unravel. I'm smiling with it. Moving with him. With the brush.

Traffic picks up. Kids and teachers coming to school. Heads turn passing us. A bus comes by. My mother isn't driving it. Yet.

Steve does the last bit. I'm tingling. Then it's *him*, not the brush, Steve's fingers working through my hair. Pulling out the waves. *His* fingers on my scalp.

I shake myself.

"Steve, thanks, huh?"

He wraps an arm around my waist. The other above my chest.

"I missed you, Angelyn. Really missed you."

"Let me go," I say. Stiff.

He pulls me in. Swirls his hips, dancing me in place.

A kiss to my neck. "I don't want no girl but you."

I roll my shoulders wildly. "Let *go*!"

Steve freezes.

"Bad touch!" one of the guys says from the sidewalk.

"How could there be with *her*?" another says.

The rest are laughing.

Steve opens his arms. "Bitch." Ragged voice.

I stumble forward, bare toes on the pavement.

"Bitch!" he calls as I cross the street.

"Bitch!" when I'm on the other side.

It follows me.

CHAPTER SEVENTEEN

"Angelyn?"

"Angelyn."

Two voices.

I lift my head from the desk. "What?"

118

Mr. Rossi is at the front of the aisle. "Class is over."

"You fell asleep," Jeni says, leaning to me from her desk.

The three of us are alone. "Did I snore?"

"Are you all right?" Mr. Rossi asks.

"No," I say. Then: "Yeah. Sure."

"Anything I can do to help?"

Jeni stands. "We should go."

I try to think. "Can we have lunch with you?"

"What?" Jeni is staring.

Mr. Rossi makes way for us. "I'm going out today, Angelyn."

I stop by him. "Where will you be?"

He smiles. A slight smile.

"I'm having nostalgia for lunch."

"We'll have that too," I say, and leave fast.

"What's *nostalgia-for-lunch*?" Jeni asks in the hall.

I'm afraid to look back. "Someplace that isn't here."

■ ■ ■

At lunchtime we wait by his car.

"Angelyn!" Jeni can't stay still. "He didn't ask us. Let's go."

"He wanted to ask," I say.

Mr. Rossi doesn't look surprised to see us. Or mad.

"Ladies." He pops the locks.

"This is *crazy*," Jeni says behind her hand.

"So's my fucking life," I say.

He takes us to a frosty in the next town, across from the state park. Off-season, we're the only customers. We stand outside in a row at the order window. The counterwoman sways to oldies rock.

"I don't have any money," I say.

Jeni says, "I'm not hungry."

"I'm buying," Mr. Rossi says. "You girls find a place to sit."

Jeni checks the space. "That won't be hard."

The dining area is four picnic tables on a concrete pad under a rusted aluminum awning. I step up to a tabletop, and Jeni takes the one opposite.

The sky is streaked with clouds. A warm breeze blows. Storm weather. Rain begins to spatter against the awning, a sound like bacon frying.

"What are we doing here?" Jeni asks.

I look at Mr. Rossi ordering. "Having lunch."

"With him."

"I ate with him yesterday after you bugged out on me."

"I did not *bug out*, Angelyn. My mom and Nathan's dad had a fight, and—"

"Whatever," I say. "I don't care. Mr. Rossi is cool. That's all."

She's quiet. "You weren't at the steps this morning."

I see myself stumbling from Steve. Hurt. I could tell her about it.

"So? I never said I'd be there every day."

Mr. Rossi comes over with a cardboard container of drinks. Hot chocolates for us and coffee for him. I thank him, taking mine, and warm my hands around it.

Jeni sets hers on the bench.

Mr. Rossi swings up beside me. Close.

"Hey," I say. Surprised. But where else would he sit?

He waves to the window. "She's got fries cooking for everyone."

My mouth waters. "I am so hungry."

"Hungry, tired, not dressed right." Mr. Rossi ticks them off.

I draw away. "Not dressed right?"

He points to my feet in flip-flops.

"I had to leave the house fast."

"Is anyone looking out for you, Angelyn?"

"I'm doing okay."

"I can see that." His voice is teasing. Light.

I cross arms over my cheap T. Feeling *less-than*.

Jeni catches my eye. "Cool?" she mouths.

The radio is playing something psychedelic.

"I used to come here in high school," Mr. Rossi says. "With the prettiest girl of the day."

I look up. "Your wife, you mean?"

"No, Angelyn." Like he's laughing. "I met *her* after high school."

"Oh."

"This was the place to be," Mr. Rossi says. "That same woman was serving. These same tunes were playing."

Jeni says, "Only they weren't oldies then."

She smiles at me. I smile back.

"Ha. Ha," Mr. Rossi says. Separate sounds. "No, Strawberry Alarm Clock was before my time. Even then."

"Strawberry *who*?" Jeni says, and now we're laughing.

Mr. Rossi sinks head in hands. "You girls are *harsh*."

"Hey, my mom likes eighties metal," I say.

Mentioning her brings it all back. I get quiet.

Rain pounds. I can smell the fries and practically taste the salt.

A new song starts. Something about rock and roll never dying.

Mr. Rossi sits up. "Aw, yeah!" He drums his thighs.

Jeni rolls her eyes.

"This is from *Grease*," he says. "You must have seen it."

I have seen it, but I don't say anything. Neither does Jeni.

"The song is from the movie," Mr. Rossi says. "Not the musical."

"Oh," Jeni says like she cares.

"We did the musical in high school. I was Danny Zuko."

"Like John Travolta in the movie?" I ask.

He turns to me. "Yeah! I was this jock too. Nobody knew I could sing."

He's nicked himself shaving. Along the jaw. "You sing, Mr. Rossi?"

"In the right mood. I haven't been there in a long time."

"Sing if you want." I'm careful not to look at Jeni. "We won't mind."

Mr. Rossi chuckles. "You may be sorry that you said that."

The song is fast and jumpy. He mumble-sings a beat behind.

"Everybody rock," he says, then sings. The words repeat and Mr. Rossi catches them, syncing his voice with the group's at the chorus.

He bounces with the music, popping shoulders, swinging his arms. His hip hits mine and then his elbow. Ducking sideways, I tip my drink, spilling most of it. My feet skid as I try to right myself. A hold on nothing, I start a fall.

In one easy move Mr. Rossi grasps my waist and upper arm, setting me upright—"'kay?"—and letting me go.

"Sorry," he says. "Now, you sing too!"

I stare at him. "I don't know the words."

"'Rock and roll'! Just keep saying it."

The song is saying it. Over and over.

I shake my head.

"Count of three," Mr. Rossi says. "Now, one, two—"

I sit forward, elbows on knees.

"Why don't you leave her alone?" Jeni says.

Mr. Rossi says, "Huh?"

"It's all right," I say.

"Angelyn?"

I frown where no one can see.

"Wait," he says. "Are you shook up from that? I thought we were having fun."

I clear my throat. "*You* were. But I can't sing."

"That was dumb of me. To push you." Like he's asking a question.

I sit up. "There's nothing wrong."

His smile wobbles. "Sure?"

"Sure," I say.

Mr. Rossi fake-wipes his forehead. "Whew."

I lean back, hands flat on the table. "Yeah, we are good."

He looks at me. My boobs. His eyes go there. I wait for it and there's no mistaking.

Mr. Rossi's eyes travel to mine. We see each other.

"Sing more," I say.

His face is flushed. "The song is over."

"Too bad," I say.

"I think the fries are done." Jeni's voice is high. Unnatural.

"I'll check." He launches from the bench.

"What's going on?" Jeni says. Hushed now.

I swipe the cup to the ground. "Nothing."

"Angelyn—I feel like something bad is happening."

"It isn't."

She checks Mr. Rossi at the order window. "Let's tell him we want to go."

"I don't want to go. Where are we supposed to go?"

"Why am *I* here?" Jeni asks. "So things will look less weird?"

"Tomorrow have lunch with Nathan," I say.

"If that's how it is, I will. I'll still tell you—I don't like this."

"Stop talking to me like a teacher."

"Someone has to!" She points to Mr. Rossi. "*He* isn't."

"I know," I say, "and that's *great* because I hate teachers."

Mr. Rossi turns. "Angelyn! Quiet back there."

Like a fistful of ice to the face.

I crash out of the table. He calls after me. I stop at the edge of the patio.

Mr. Rossi comes up behind. "Hey."

I take a breath. "Why'd you have to yell? I had your back."

"What?"

I look around. "She was going off on you. I had your back."

Mr. Rossi is frowning. "I think you picked up the wrong idea about me."

I shrug. "Okay."

"The singing and all—that was me being goofy. I'm in a funny mood."

"Hey, me too."

"I don't understand this. I knocked into you—I said I was sorry. You spilled your drink. Of course, I'll get you another one."

"It's not any of that," I say sharply.

"Look," Mr. Rossi says. "Just now—"

"It's all right. It's all right. I said things are good. I meant it."

I don't want to hear him lie.

I face the street. The little gray house across.

"Mr. Rossi, don't ever *not-like* me."

"*Not-like* you? Angelyn, I like you. As a student. A kid."

"I know you like me. I know it for sure. Just don't stop."

"Why would I stop?" he asks.

"Because everyone does. Only not you. Okay?"

He doesn't answer. Does not answer.

The counterwoman calls, "Order up!"

The rain hits the awning like rocks.

CHAPTER EIGHTEEN

After school I take the bus home. It's near dark when I step out. The houses along the way are shut tight, lights off or faint behind blinds.

Passing Mrs. Daly's old place, I let myself look. It's run-down, a rental, the fence gone, a driveway in its place. The yard paved to hold a makeshift garage. I remember being in that yard on a blanket in the grass, doing homework while Mrs. Daly tended roses and her dog Brandy slept nearby. The bushes are there still, vines brown and twisted on the side of the house.

Our place is cold. Mom and Danny's breakfast dishes are stacked in the sink.

I look through the kitchen for a note. A number where she's at. Money for food. A sign they're coming back. I don't find anything. I check the rest of the house. Nothing. No messages on the phone.

Back in the kitchen I do a snap-fingered dance. "Party time!"

Not enough friends for a game of two square.

I find random food—a peach, cheddar popcorn—and eat it at the sink.

The front room is Danny's world. The big TV and the couch

facing it. He's hardly left a dent in the cushions with his long, lean body. The couch smells of him: beer-sweat and tobacco. I take an edge and watch a *Simpsons* from there. All the while I feel that Danny's behind me. I know he isn't, but I hold that same inch of couch. Until the show is over.

The house echoes with quiet.

I am not grounded. No one's cared to ground me.

I call Steve.

"Um" is what he says when I ask him over.

I pace with the phone. "Forget the stuff this morning. I have."

His cell crackles. "Angelyn, you can't knock me around like that."

I swallow hard. "Yeah."

"Why should I come?" Steve asks.

"Because I'm here."

No answer. I wait and wait.

"Steve?"

"Twenty minutes," he says.

In his quilted jacket and big boots, Steve shrinks the room.

"You live in a dump," he says. Turning, staring.

I fold my arms. "Uh-huh."

"It's cold here." His nose wrinkles. "It *stinks*."

"Okay, Steve. I'm poor. Is that all right?"

He faces me. "Is this why you never asked me over?"

"Yeah, and—well, you saw them. The people I live with."

He nods. "Your mom and him are gone, you said."

"For the weekend."

"What'd you have in mind, Angelyn?"

"I don't know. We could go out. See a movie. Maybe get some food."

He's shaking his head. "I didn't come here to be your ride."

"Steve—"

"Not that kind of ride."

Despite it all, I smile. "You're disgusting."

He cracks a grin. "And you love it."

"So," I say. "You want to *do it* and leave?"

"No, I don't want to 'do it and leave.' Not if we've got the weekend. I will stay. But why can't we have dessert first?"

"Dessert?" I'm groaning.

"Yeah. There's something in it for you, Ange. I'll show you what."

I rub my arms. "We'd go out after?"

Steve steps to me. "Whatever you want."

Inches apart, we stare. He takes my wrists and pulls me toward the couch.

I slip free. "We don't want that grungy thing."

"Where, then?"

"Your truck? We could park."

He slaps his thigh. "Here we've got a house and no parents—"

"Danny is not my parent."

"No *adults*," Steve says. "For tonight and all the way to Sunday. Right?"

I lean against the doorframe. "Right."

"You said you didn't want to be alone." He points to himself. "I'm here."

"Only not on the couch," I say.

I let him lead me to another room. Mom and Danny's room. Steve sits me on their bed. I think that I can do it—that it won't matter. I stretch with him across the comforter.

His fingers tap my zipper. He's pushing. Pressing. And I'm pulling off my shirt like I want *it*—whatever *it* is—as badly as he does.

"You are going to love this," Steve says.

I pull him to me. He fumbles with my bra clasp.

"I will," I say, and while I do, he rears off to strip himself.

Arms above my head. The bra sliding from my finger to the floor.

"Angelyn," he says. Choked. And falls on me.

Bare chests pressed, we roll on the cool and shiny polyester.

"Let's get under the covers," Steve says.

"What?"

He's pulling me up. Tossing the comforter back.

"Steve—"

The bed is unmade underneath. Bunched blankets, rumpled sheets.

He rummages through like he's making us a nest.

Danny's musk is rising. A long black hair from Mom sticks against a pillow.

I want to spew.

"Not here either." I backstep from the bed. "Don't even get mad."

Steve faces me. "You know, you're not Goldilocks."

"Yeah, well." I nod to him. "I don't think *that* is what she was looking for."

"Okay. Where do *you* sleep?"

We shuffle down the hall, me topless in jeans, Steve naked.

"Here." I point.

He snaps on the light. I wince at the bright overhead.

Silence, then: "What are you, *ten*?"

I see my room as Steve does. Twin bed. Plain frame desk and a straight chair stacked with clothes. Walls bare except for a high shelf that holds my model horses. Sixteen in a row, watching the bed. Watching over me.

Steve is laughing. "Hot-ass Angelyn and this is how you live. Wild."

"So *this one* isn't right for you?" I ask, arm anchored across my breasts.

"Hey, no." He turns. "It's fine. It's a bed, isn't it?"

"Yes. It's a bed."

He smooths a hand along the mattress. "This could work."

"Why wouldn't it?" I ask.

Steve grins. "Wish I'd known you back then."

I gawk at him. "When I was *ten*?"

"Well, no." He walks to me. "Not ten." Steve pets my arm.

I let it drop. "Didn't think so."

"Yeah," he says, holding me. "Not ten."

We're moving to the bed.

"Twelve, say."

I freeze against him. "What?"

"Yeah. You're twelve and I'm fourteen. Doin' homework."

"Okay, stop."

Steve laughs to himself. "Your freaky folks down the hall—"

"Hey!"

He nuzzles me. "You're this hot little girl."

Palms out, I shove him off.

Steve stumbles backward, hard onto the bed.

"Angelyn, what the hell!"

I'm tugging on a T-shirt. "Don't *talk* that way."

He squints. "So, now it's off."

"Thanks to you," I say.

"You are crazy. You know that? Crazy."

Steve stomps out.

The walls close in.

"Why does everything have to be about *that*?" I say down the hall.

He pops out of their room, kicking on his jeans.

"You brought me here for *that*," he says. "*That* is why I came."

I flap a hand. "Why can't we watch TV? Or, I don't know—talk."

Steve ducks into the room again. He steps out dressed.

"Okay. Tell me what just happened."

"What do you mean?" I ask.

"Why'd you get so weird? Let's talk about that."

I press to the wall. "You were being gross."

"'Gross.' Good one, Angelyn."

"Stay anyway?" I ask, small-voiced.

"Stay and then what?"

"I don't know. Just stay."

"I'm out," Steve says. But doesn't move.

"We can talk!" I say. "I'll talk."

"I don't believe you," he says. "But, okay—go."

Oh God. "I can't—be with you that way here."

Steve all but taps his foot. "I get that. Why?"

I bite the inside of my cheek. I shut my eyes.

He would tell. Everyone.

And:

I don't have the words anyway.

I open my eyes. Steve is staring.

"Angelyn?" His voice is a little softer.

"You can go," I say.

"What?"

"You were right, Steve. You should go."

His face closes. "You are going to end up alone. I mean, like, forever."

"Yeah," I say, like: *I do not give a shit.*

Steve leaves.

I wait five minutes and I leave too.

CHAPTER NINETEEN

I stay to the ditch that parallels the connector road to the high-way. I watch for Steve's headlights, but I don't see his or any-one's. It's full dark, and I move from memory, one foot after the other through scrub brush.

At the highway I tuck my hair in my collar, hoping I pass as a guy. I walk along the shoulder, cars and trucks whipping by. A group in a van comes honking next to me. I wave them on.

Off the highway I pass the county fairgrounds. My shirt is sopping and my mouth is dry. A sign by a driveway reads "Blue Creek Care Home." I read it more than once. Mrs. Daly's place, Jeni said.

In town the bars and restaurants are busy, loud talk and laughs spilling out. Pickups cruise. Friday night. I move through like a ghost. A thirsty ghost.

Farther along Main, everything's shut. I pass auto fix-its, a nail salon, a TV repair shop. My legs ache and still I'm miles away. I think about calling him.

He'd tell me *no*. He'd have to say that.

A minimart lights the next block. I don't have a cent, but I make it my goal.

The clerk is hard-faced with pencil brows.

"All I need is a cup," I say. "Water's free, right?"

She shakes her head. "They'd charge us for inventory."

I point toward the drinks machine. Row after row of cups.

"Nobody ever messes up and has to take a second one?"

"Nothing here is free," the clerk says.

I put out my hand. "The key to the bathroom."

She smirks. "Bathroom's for customers only."

I lean on the counter. "Please. I just want something to drink."

She checks the closed-circuit. "Move along, hon."

"Don't call me *hon*."

The door opens with a cheery ring.

The clerk looks past. "Yes, *sir*. How can I help you?"

I stand there out of ideas.

The guy walks up. "Angelyn, hey. I thought that was you."

Nathan Daly.

I stare at him.

"Thirty bucks gas," he says, handing over a couple of twenties.

"Where'd you get that money?" I ask.

Nathan shrugs. "Working. I'm in town delivering wood."

I swallow dry. "Feel like doing me a favor?"

He smiles widely. "Name it."

Nathan pumps gas while I chug a soda next to the truck.

Fluorescent lights thrum above us. Moths flutter.

I run a hand over the primered hood. "Yours?"

"My dad's," Nathan says. "I'm driving it these days."

"Nice," I say. Nodding.

"I saw you in town," he says.

"You followed me here?"

Nathan glances up. "Well, I needed gas."

I nod again, mechanically.

He sets the nozzle back. "You all right, Angelyn?"

I hoist the near-empty soda. "I owe you for this."

"No problem."

"The thing is, there's something more."

We drive in and out of cloud cover, a full moon behind it.

Nathan looks over. "I wish you'd say where we're going."

"Where *I'm* going. Left turn coming up."

He swings onto the road that runs by our old grade school.

"You promised not to ask," I remind him.

"Okay. I won't ask about *that.*"

I settle on the patched seat. "Good."

"But why are you out by yourself?"

"Nathan."

"It's a different question."

We crest a hill and there's Blue Creek Elementary.

"Remember that place?" he asks.

"Yeah. It was shitty there."

"You would call me *retard* and such. You and your friends."

"We weren't the only ones," I say.

"Angelyn, you didn't start until I told about your stepdad."

I tap a nail on the window. "Not that again."

Nathan leans with the wheel like he's steering a ship.

"There's something I never got straight."

"Watch the road, huh?"

He coasts to a Stop sign. "Which way?"

Left is town. Right is the country. I point right.

"Who do you know out here?" Nathan asks.

"No one you do."

Forest on both sides. No light but the truck's. No signs.

I look in all directions, trying to place us.

"Do you know where we're going?" Nathan asks.

"Just drive, okay?"

We jump along the road. Dark miles.

The forest thins, cut by driveways. House lights beyond the trees.

"It could be soon," I say.

"Tell me when." Nathan sounds pissed.

I see the white arch over the driveway. The horse at its center.

"There," I call, throwing my arm out hard.

Nathan swings the truck in.

"Stop!" I say, and he shuts it down.

Ahead the drive curves out of sight. Crickets chirp in tall oleander.

"Lights off," I say.

We sit in the dark.

"Why'd I bring you here?" Nathan asks.

I'm working up my nerve to leave.

"Angelyn. Tell me one thing. It's all I want to know."

I rest my head on the seatback. "Is that the price of the ride?"

"The price?" Nathan says. "Sure, I guess."

Tired, I say, "Ask."

He clears his throat. "Why'd you hate me for telling the truth?"

"The truth." I take a moment. "You mean what you saw at my house?"

"Yeah."

"Nathan. You know what happened after 'the truth.' The cops came, and I had to talk to them. We all did."

"You lied to them," he says.

I lift my shoulders. "Call it that. I don't care. My mom was mad. *So* mad."

Nathan says, "We could hear her yelling."

"Right, and then I couldn't see your grandma anymore."

"Or me," he says.

I roll my eyes. "I was alone with them—Mom, Danny, and me—and it was *all* on me. Mom's never stopped being mad."

"But did *he* stop?"

I look in Nathan's direction. "What?"

"Your stepdad stopped when I told. Didn't he?"

"Yeah." My voice is flat.

"Well, that was good. Wasn't it?"

I don't answer.

"Your stepdad was hurting you," Nathan says. "I stopped him."

"He wasn't hurting me."

"He'd hold you tight—like a wrestler—and then he'd hit at you."

"Hit at me?" I laugh. "Is that what you thought he was doing?"

"I saw him touch between your legs."

"Shut up," I say.

"You couldn't have stopped him, Angelyn. He wouldn't have stopped himself."

"It wasn't up to *you*!"

Nathan is quiet. "My mom used to hit me. So, I know."

"Don't be dumb," I say. "It's not the same thing."

"A neighbor reported her. That's how I came to live with Grandma."

"Nathan, I remember. Why go over it?"

"I know you remember. Because you and me were friends."

I stare out at nothing. "Don't."

"We'd play Monopoly. Remember that? And cards. Grandma would make us cookies. Oatmeal chocolate chip. She'd help us with our homework."

Afternoons, after school. "Yes," I say.

"Saturdays, I'd go to church with Grandma," Nathan says. "Sundays, she'd be at church club and I'd stay home. I'd play on the roof, under this tree that hung there."

My face burns. "Is that where you did your peeping?"

Nathan says, "Yeah. I saw you guys."

"Did you like the show?"

"No. From the first time, I wanted to tell."

"Why didn't you?"

I hear him breathing.

"I was scared I'd lose my place."

"What?"

"Grandma would take you in like she took me. I'd be out."

I shake my head. "That never would have happened."

"There wasn't hardly room for me, Angelyn. There'd be no room for you."

"Listen. Mom never would have let Mrs. Daly take me."

"It's what I thought then," Nathan says. "So, I kept quiet. I'm sorry. I've been sorry."

His voice is thick. I turn it over, what he said.

"That's why you've been following—*stalking* me? To say you're sorry?"

"Not stalking. And, yeah. But not only that."

"You don't need to say *sorry*. Anyway, you told what you saw. You did tell."

"I had to. He was getting worse. He'd be making faces behind you. Rubbing on himself."

I sit up. "I don't want to know that!"

"Angelyn, I'm dropping out next month when I turn eighteen. I'm never going to pass those tests for graduation."

I shrug and remember he can't see. "Oh," I say.

"I've been wanting to know that you're okay. That you'll *be* okay."

"Without you, you mean?" I want to laugh. Wildly. I can't get the sound out.

Nathan says, "I don't mean that. I've been wondering about you for a long time. Pretty soon I won't be around even to have the chance to ask."

"Well, things are crazy, but they're always crazy. I don't know how I'll be later. Nobody knows that."

"Your stepdad ought to be gone. Whether he stopped or not."

"I talked to her about Danny," I say. "Just a little. All Mom did was blow up—again."

"Your mom still thinks he didn't touch you?"

"I don't know what she thinks. Anything I say to Mom, it's automatically wrong."

"Make it matter to her, Angelyn. Tell her up front."

I remember where I'm at. "Okay, I answered way more than one question."

"Wait. Don't go!" All panicked.

I haven't moved. "What do you want from me, Nathan?"

In the dark our hands scrape.

Cool settles on me. I grip his hand and lean across. Find his mouth and press mine to it.

Like kissing a statue. If statues shook.

I sit back. "Are we good now?"

Nathan leans to me. He winds fingers in my hair. They smell like gas. He holds my head like it's something precious.

"*No.*" But I don't say it. In shock, I say nothing at all.

Nathan kisses me. He's gentle. Clumsy. Just outside the lines.

I open my mouth. Our tongues bump. He pulls away.

"Angelyn! Wow." A laugh behind his words and something tender.

"You're the same as Danny."

"Huh?"

I pet Nathan's lap like a dog. His hips rise to meet my hand.

"You see?" I let it hover.

We sit in our separate corners.

"Why did you do that?" he asks.

I strain ahead to see—anything. "To show you."

"Show me what?"

"I know what you want, and that's it."

"Angelyn, you kissed me first."

"To kiss you *off*," I say. "You put your hands all over me."

"I did not!" He stops. "Not like that. I just like you. I always have."

"Danny liked me."

Nathan swears. It sounds wrong, coming from him.

"I am not your stepdad! It is not the same."

"It's the same!" I say. "Congratulations. You're normal."

"Why are you so mean to me?" he asks.

"I'm not being mean. I'm being real."

"You weren't being real," he says, "when you kissed me."

I work my shoulders. "No."

Heavy quiet.

"You hate me," Nathan says. "You hate me right now. You hate me still."

I check outside, my eyes adjusting. "I'm getting out."

"What is this place?" he asks. "What are you going to do here?"

"I don't know." A shiver runs through me. "That's your last question."

"No. One more. When are you going to see my grandma?"

"Oh, Nathan. Stop it."

"She was your friend too. She helped me understand things, and you too."

"We're grown-up now," I say.

"See her." Nathan's voice is dull.

"Thanks for the ride."

"I always thought you were so pretty," he says.

I step down. Nathan throws the truck in reverse. I watch him go.

Shaking.

CHAPTER TWENTY

My sneakered feet crunch gravel down the drive. I run a hand
along the oleander, holding the leaves and letting them go.

A dog is barking, closing in.

Dark shape coming at me.

I crouch. "Dolly! Dolly, girl."

She knocks me flat. And licks me to death.

Dolly stays until a whistle calls her off. I walk on.

The house is lit. Mr. Rossi's on the porch steps, shirtless,
in shorts. Dolly jumps in front, telling a story in short, breathy
barks.

I reach the pool. Lights flood. A motion sensor.

Mr. Rossi stands. "Who's there?"

"Me," I say. "Angelyn."

He shades his eyes. "From school?"

I stop at the walkway. "Yes, me."

Beer cans line the step behind him.

Mr. Rossi follows my look. "I was just—"

"Drinking," I say. "It's all right."

His leg brushes a can, tipping it. The can rolls down the steps with a tinny rattle. Mr. Rossi lunges for it, stooping to gather the rest.

I don't know where to look. I'm working not to laugh.

He props the screen door with an elbow, arms full. "Wait outside."

My laughs bubble over when he's in. I snort them in my hands.

Dolly circles, whimpering.

I bend to her. "Silly dog."

She's sleek. Meat on her bones. Her eyes are bright.

He's taken care.

144

"Love you," I say. Dolly smiles.

I lie on the lawn, arms behind my head, watching the house. I flex my feet in ratty sneakers. My jeans are gritty; my T-shirt, stretched and smelly. I think about his wife—of the yellow, silky tank—and wonder what she looks like.

Something rustles in the grass. Dolly bolts and I'm up and shuddering. On tiptoes I run past the garage to the tire swing. Climbing in feels like safety. The rope twists. The tire turns. I shut my eyes.

Another tire swing, my mother in shorts and tank top. She runs me backward and lets go. I fly away laughing, legs out straight. "Brave girl," she calls.

"What are you doing here, Angelyn?"

In T-shirt and jeans, Mr. Rossi stands opposite in the clearing.

"You changed," I say, lifting the tire around me like a donut.

"Why'd you come?"

"This stuff happened," I say.

"What if my wife were here? How would I explain you?"

I drop the tire and sit in it. "She isn't, though."

"How do you know that?"

"Mr. Rossi, you said she left you."

He stumbles on something. "And, what? You're here to take her place?"

I stop moving. "I thought it would be—easier—if she weren't here."

"You thought what would be easier?"

I look past him to the house. "For me to visit you."

Mr. Rossi looks with me. "Angelyn, you're not staying."

"Why?" I ask. "Nobody's home. We brought Dolly here."

He slams his chest. "*I'm* home. The dog was a mistake."

"She is not! You said she was working out."

"I want you to leave," Mr. Rossi says.

I grip the tire. "Maybe I'll go, and maybe I'll take her with me."

He stands there. Unsteady.

Getting out of the tire is harder than getting in. My feet tangle and I fall backward, landing in the dirt with a *whumpf.*

Mr. Rossi says my name—pissed, not worried.

I gather breath. "I'm going."

"I don't need this," he says as I push myself up.

"Mr. Rossi, I can smell it on you," I say, hobbling past.

"This is my home," he says. Loud. "I do what I want."

Back at the driveway, I call for Dolly.

"What do you think you're doing?" Mr. Rossi says behind me.

I jump. And start away.

"Where are you going now?"

"I don't know," I say. "Somewhere! I'll catch a ride. Hitch."

"Stop right there. You are not hitchhiking."

I face the dark.

"Are you in some kind of trouble, Angelyn?"

"Every day of my life."

"What do you want me to do about it?" Mr. Rossi asks.

I lift a shoulder. "I needed a place to be. I thought it could be here."

"So you show up on my doorstep like some refugee?"

I turn. "Oh, I'm too dirty for you? Still not dressed right?"

Mr. Rossi walks at me. "Simmer down."

I walk backward. "I'll wash, then. My clothes and me."

He stops. "What are you talking about?"

I'm kicking off shoes. Tugging at my shirt.

"Don't—do not—take off your clothes."

"Why not?" My voice catches. "You don't like them. You keep saying."

"Angelyn!"

I run from him.

Gravel stings my feet. I dig in harder. The motion sensor spreads light, and I aim for the center of it. My feet slap grass and cool concrete, then—*hard, cold water* as I cannonball into the pool.

Sinking, I unwrap arms and legs. The water is clouded, the light above filtered through a crust. I paddle underneath, staring at the surface. The view doesn't change. He doesn't come. My eyes burn. Cheeks puff. My heart beats in my ears.

My toenails scrape bottom. It's silty. Freezing. I lift them, writhing.

The pool goes dark.

I gasp and water pushes in. Cold sweeps me and I hang frozen.

The light comes back. I see Dolly's shadow. Her bark reaches me.

I push off from the bottom and arrow to the top.

Spitting water, I grip the pool ledge. Dolly races around.

Leaves and twigs carpet the water, moving with me like we're part of some cold soup. I cycle my legs for heat, my jeans tightening like bandages.

Something lights on my arm. A giant moth, walking dazed. I swallow a scream and shake it off. The moth leaves lopsided, Dolly snapping after it. Under my hand the gutter is lined with bugs that weren't so lucky.

"Nice pool," I shout, lifting out of it.

"Can you swim?" Mr. Rossi from a distance. Slurred words.

I squelch toward the house, stopping once to peel a leaf off my foot.

He's on the porch, sprawled across a brown wicker couch.

"Yes," I say, climbing the steps. "I can swim."

"No one uses the pool."

"*I* used it." I'm trembling. "Now I'm taking a shower. *In your house.*"

Mr. Rossi flaps a hand like, really, he couldn't care.

I run the shower scalding and take my time. After, naked in the steamy small room, I toe my wrecked clothes to a corner and reach for hers. The yellow tank, still there. Yoga pants from a basket of exercise clothes. A green jacket from a hook behind the door. It's fleece and warms my shoulders like a hug. I towel-dry my hair. Put on socks.

Mr. Rossi is how I left him. At his feet, Dolly thumps her tail.

I stand in front.

He looks up. "Feel better?"

"Yes," I say. I do.

"I couldn't go after you, Angelyn."

"Because you're drunk," I say.

"Yes," Mr. Rossi says. "I can't drive you home either."

"Guess I'll have to stay."

"Your parents will be worried."

"My 'parents' are gone for the weekend. The whole weekend."

"Who else can you call?"

"Mr. Rossi, can't you see there's no one?"

He struggles to sit up. "I'll call a cab."

"Why can't I just *be* here? I'm not hurting anyone."

Our eyes meet.

"You know why," he says.

"I'll sleep outside. In the *garage*, even."

Mr. Rossi says, "No," in a way to end all arguments.

I move from him along the whitewashed boards. "You're like all of them."

"All of who?"

"*Them!* People. *Friends.* Things get tough and you don't want to know me."

"I'm not like that," he says.

I walk back. "Let me stay one night."

"You know I can't."

"You're *scared* to let me stay. Scared I'm this big slut."

Mr. Rossi looks at me. "I don't know anything about that."

I'm trying not to cry. "What is so wrong with me?"

"You think you're the only one who's having a bad night, Angelyn?"

I push my hair back. Pain on his face. I sink against the rail.

"What's wrong with you?" I ask.

Mr. Rossi brings out chips and soda for us, dog food for Dolly.

"You do like her," I say as he sets her bowl on the porch.

Tail wagging, Dolly attacks it. Mr. Rossi scratches between her shoulders.

"Hey, I need all the friends I can get."

We sit on the couch, the bag of chips between us.

"Thanks," I say, taking some. "I know I'm a problem."

Mr. Rossi is smiling. I ask what's funny.

"I was picturing the police—the principal—*my wife*—driving in and finding you here in those clothes and me like this."

My chest is tight. "The police?"

"I almost called them while I was inside," Mr. Rossi says.

"What?" I say, sick. "Why? I'll leave now if it's like that."

"I didn't call. I don't have the energy to explain anything to anyone."

"Mr. Rossi, there's nothing to explain. I told you—you don't have to worry about me."

"You came by on the worst night of my life, Angelyn. One of them."

I watch him. "Worse than mine? I doubt it."

"Try this. Today is my son's birthday. He's four. I called where they're at, and my wife wouldn't bring him to the phone. I heard party sounds in the background."

I sit back. "That is bad. I bet he misses you."

"She says I won't see Camden again."

"Your wife says—what?"

Mr. Rossi covers his eyes. "I think you heard me."

"Can she do that?"

"Who knows? She thinks she can."

"Mr. Rossi, what did you do?"

He looks at me.

"I mean—" Faltering. "Why is she so pissed?"

"What I did is not up for discussion."

"Okay."

We're quiet.

Mr. Rossi pushes the chip bag to me. "Want more?"

"Maybe later."

He sets the bag in an empty plant stand and leans back, legs outstretched.

"What's your story tonight, Angelyn?"

The whole mess spreads before me. Mom. Danny. Steve. Nathan.

"Can I say *it's not up for discussion*?"

Mr. Rossi laughs. "Yeah. Heck, yeah!"

But I tell him a little.

"This guy—the one who brought me here—"

Mr. Rossi frowns.

"He didn't know where he was at. Anyway, this guy can't do enough for me. Nathan is all about *helping*. So, tonight, first chance he gets, he's—*Mr. Hands.* I knew it was that. I just knew it. When I called him on it, he brought out his grandma. Yeah, Nathan. Smooth. At least with Steve, you know right off what *he* wants."

Mr. Rossi is quiet a long time. "Nathan's grandma. Someone you know?"

"She was my neighbor. She's in a nursing home now. He wants me to see her."

"Is this the neighbor who helped you after school?"

I smile, happy—*amazed*—that he remembered. "That's her. Mrs. Daly."

"You loved her," Mr. Rossi says.

"Yes."

"I'm with Nathan. See her."

"But, Mr. Rossi, he doesn't mean it. He's using her to get to me."

"Look, maybe this kid wants to get with you *and* wants you to see his grandma. One thing doesn't have to block the other. Things are generally more complicated than that."

Mr. Rossi's serious expression stretches to a yawn.

"I'll fall asleep out here if I'm not careful."

"Don't go in," I say. "Tell me about Blue Creek High when you were there."

"Oh. Well," Mr. Rossi says. "It hasn't changed all that much. Ten years, more or less. Miss Bass was an English teacher then. One of my teachers."

"She was? Were the groups the same—the cowboys, the jocks, and all?"

"We hardly noticed the cowboys," he says. "They had their corner, and we had—the rest of the school, I guess. I was a jock. A rich kid, you'd say. I had the grades too. My friends were like me, and we all stayed together."

"It's like that now," I say. "The cowboys don't have much to do with the prep kids. Some of the people Steve knows have money. They've got the tallest trucks, the biggest cabs, the best sound systems. Everything's new. Steve's folks have money too, but they dime it out to him. That's what he says. Nobody cares much about school."

Mr. Rossi's head is turned to me. "How do you fit into that world, Angelyn?"

"It's Steve's call if I'm in it or not. I'm out now."

"But do you want to be in it?"

I face him. *"They'd* say I'm with Steve or I'm nowhere."

"They're wrong," Mr. Rossi says. "All of that fades, and fast. It's high school. Ten years ago, I thought I'd be someplace way different than I'm at now."

"Where did you think you'd be?"

"Playing baseball! Angelyn, you'd see me on TV."

I think of Danny. "So, why aren't you playing baseball?"

"I was good," Mr. Rossi says. "Good enough to get a scholarship to play for Stanford, no less. I played infield. Freshman year was great. Sophomore year, I tore a ligament in my knee. I had surgery and rehab. Two games back, I tore it again. I was never as good after that. I wasn't good enough."

"Did they kick you out of Stanford, Mr. Rossi?"

He smiles at me. "No. Just off the team. I stayed and got my teaching credential. My mom told me she was just as proud."

"I'd be proud of you," I say.

Mr. Rossi looks off. Standing, he crosses to the column by the steps.

"I used to sit out here with her."

I try to see him little. "You did?"

"All the time. We'd watch the stars and talk about anything."

"My mom and I don't talk. We fight."

"Mine understood me. Wanted the best for me. Thought I was the best."

I curl into the couch. "Must be nice."

"That part of my life is over, Angelyn. I can't ever get it back."

"Why?" I whisper, fixed on him.

"She died when I was twenty-three."

"Oh no."

"A plane crash. My stepfather's plane. He died too."

"I'm sorry. Sorry."

His eyes glint.

"Was it a good time for you," he asks, "when you knew Mrs. Daly?"

"Yes," I say. "It was."

"Go back there, Angelyn. I wish I could. See that lady while you can."

"I'll go if you'll take me." I say the words as I think them.

Mr. Rossi goes into the house.

I watch after. And wait. He doesn't come back.

I feel like—nothing. No. Sad. So sad.

I try to guess the time. Could be eleven. Could be two a.m. His property is a carpet of unbroken dark. Sound of crickets everywhere.

Dolly's left too.

I tug a throw pillow from behind and set it at my head. Pretzeled against the cold, I zip the jacket and work my hands into the sleeves.

I know that I won't sleep.

The screen door creaks. Mr. Rossi steps out with a blanket. I unbend. "Oh."

He shakes the blanket out and hands it to me.

"Thanks." I clear my throat. "Stay, Mr. Rossi."

He wobbles. "Can't."

"It will be all right," I say.

Mr. Rossi sort of falls onto the couch.

I lift the blanket. "We can share."

He pats it to my side. "This is for you."

I snuggle in. "You're the best."

"Ha. No," Mr. Rossi says.

"To me you are."

He rests his head against the wall. "You're very young."

"I know about guys."

"I'm a teacher. Not a guy."

I hide a smile. "You can be both."

"Mmm."

"Mr. Rossi?"

His eyes are shut.

"I saw how you looked at me at the frosty."

He's quiet.

"You don't have to pretend. I'm okay with it."

His breaths become sighs, then snorts.

I study him. "Are you really—really sleeping?"

Mr. Rossi twitches, frowns.

"Are you cold? Aren't you cold?"

By inches I pull the blanket free. I gather a length and flip it over him.

He drags in a breath and coughs it out.

When Mr. Rossi is quiet, I edge to him until our shoulders touch.

Under the blanket our warmth combines.

Fists curled, knees tucked, I lean against him.

Mr. Rossi lifts an arm. I freeze.

He wraps it around, pulling me in.

Spread across his chest, I can hear his heart beat.

I slip arms around his waist. Smiling.

Sleepy.

CHAPTER TWENTY-ONE

I wake alone, stretched along the couch. It's daylight; cool, clear morning.

"Mr. Rossi?" I'm hoarse-voiced. Teeth fuzzy.

Dolly barks from the lawn.

The screen door creaks. "Angelyn, come in."

We stand in the hall. The floor is cold even in stocking feet.

"Your clothes are in the bathroom. I ran them through the washer and dryer. Your shoes are there too. I picked them off the lawn."

"You didn't sleep like I did."

His eyes flick over me. "I slept fine. It's time to get moving."

Moving where? I wonder. "What time is it?"

"Almost ten-thirty," Mr. Rossi says.

"You have someplace to be?"

"Got to get going," he says. Looking somewhere else.

I ask if I can take another shower.

"You do that," Mr. Rossi says. "I'll make us some breakfast."

We eat on the porch at a table with a frosted glass top. Bacon, toast, orange juice. Coffee for him.

"This is good," I say. "Like we're at a restaurant or something."

He chews dry toast. "Glad you like it."

"You've been great."

"Last night is sort of a blur," Mr. Rossi says.

"We sat on the porch. Talked. We fell asleep."

"Together," he says.

"Like friends," I say.

Mr. Rossi rubs his face.

"About your son—"

"I talked about that?" He's wincing.

"You'll see him again. I know it."

"These are private matters," Mr. Rossi says.

"I won't tell anyone. I swear I won't."

He looks at me wild-eyed. "I was impaired last night!"

Impaired? I want to laugh. I *would* laugh if it weren't for his expression.

"Mr. Rossi, you were fine. You really were."

He pushes back from the table. "It's time to take you home."

"We'll stop at Mrs. Daly's?"

"Mrs. who?"

I make my voice calm. "You remember."

Mr. Rossi takes a moment. "Your neighbor lady tutor person."

I nod. "She's in a nursing home. It's on the way. You said, *See her.*"

"All right," he says.

■ ■ ■

We sit in the parking lot.

"I'm afraid to go in," I say. "Will she even know me?"

"Nursing homes are tough," Mr. Rossi says.

"Nathan visits. Jeni sees her. If *they* can—"

"You will handle whatever you find. You're a brave kid."

Instant smile. "I am?"

"You are," he says. "Now, go. Tell her what you need to tell her."

From outside, the home looks like a budget motel, a long rectangle of rooms behind sliding glass doors. On one side of the building, a rose-lined path. On the other, a picnic area with patio furniture, a barbecue pit, and flowering planters. A calico cat is curled asleep in a lounge chair.

Through the lobby door I watch the scene inside. A nurse at a counter pages through a thick binder. Across from her, a tiny old woman and a heavy old man sit in wheelchairs against a wall.

The woman could be Mrs. Daly. I step back.

"Angelyn!"

Jeni's at the door in white pants and floral smock.

"Come in," she says with a smile I've never seen.

The smell about knocks me out, human and chemical combined.

"God," I say. The old people look over. The nurse too.

"You get used to it," Jeni says. Quietly. Kindly.

"Where is Mrs. Daly?" I ask.

"She's in Activities. Come on. I'll take you."

The room is big and sunny, walls of windows on three sides.

A dark-haired woman with a beach ball stands at the center of a circle of people in wheelchairs.

"Bill," she says, tossing to a man with muscled arms and frozen face. He catches the ball and squeezes fit to burst.

The woman walks to him. "Nice job!" She works the ball free.

"Sad," I say. "Which one is Mrs. Daly?"

"Not sad," Jeni says. "Just life. She's at the window."

Hunched in a wheelchair, Mrs. Daly looks out on a view of the picnic area. Short white hair in curls, a wrap around her shoulders.

"Wow," I say softly.

I follow Jeni there.

She leans in, a hand on Mrs. Daly's arm. "A friend is here to see you."

Mrs. Daly asks, "Who?" in a cracked little voice.

Jeni steps aside. "It's me," I say. "Angelyn."

She's smaller than I remember. Only three years, but so much older.

"We were neighbors," I say.

Mrs. Daly's smile is polite. Nothing more.

I crouch by the chair. "Angelyn Stark."

We look at each other. I recognize her eyes, clear hazel-gray.

"The little girl next door," Mrs. Daly says. Then: "Angelyn!"

I sit on my heels. "Yes. Not so little now."

"Pretty girl. I've changed, haven't I?"

I nod. "Why are you in that chair, Mrs. Daly?"

She considers herself. "Well, I don't know. Do you?"

"No," I say. Smiling.

Mrs. Daly lifts her hands. Drops them. "Are you all right?"

"I'm okay. Have you been asking for me?"

She frowns. "Have I? I am glad to see you."

"Nathan said you *had* to see me."

Her face lights. "Nathan? Is he here?"

"It's not lunch yet," Jeni says. "Let's go outside."

I stare at her. "Yeah. Let's go out."

I push Mrs. Daly along the rose path.

161

"I have heard her talk about you," Jeni says. "That wasn't a lie."

"Not quite how Nathan said, though, was it?" I keep my voice low.

She scuffs some leaves. "Maybe he wanted—"

"Oh, I'm pretty sure what Nathan wanted."

Mrs. Daly touches a yellow rose. She lifts her face to the sun.

"I'm not sorry I'm here," I say.

In back, flower boxes border a postage-stamp lawn. I set Mrs. Daly next to one and sit on it beside her. Jeni hovers.

The cat comes around, meowing.

"She's hungry," Mrs. Daly says.

"I'll get her food," Jeni says.

The cat rubs its cheek along Mrs. Daly's footpads.

"Mora lives here," she says, looking down at the cat. "Like me."

"I have a dog," I say. "Sort of."

"I am glad you came," Mrs. Daly says. "Nathan visits. My son hardly does."

"You and Nathan left our block to live with him."

"Yes," she says. "We lived with Roger."

I pick at my jeans. "You left because of me."

"Oh, I don't think so."

"You don't remember. Maybe it's good you don't remember."

"You were a child," Mrs. Daly says.

"Nathan told you something about me. I said he lied, but it was true."

"I've never known Nathan to lie," she says.

"*I* lied." Mora the cat skitters off. "My stepdad lied, and I backed him up."

First time I've said it out loud. Out right.

"Mrs. Daly, I lied to the cops. I lied to this lady they made me see. Danny and Mom weren't even there, and I kept on lying."

"You look sad," she says.

"So much is wrong," I say. "I don't know how to fix it."

"Some things aren't fixable," Mrs. Daly says.

I stiffen at that. "Do you even know what I'm talking about?"

"Yes, Angelyn. I know." Her eyes are sharp. I believe her.

"It was you who called the cops. We were supposed to hate you."

"Hate," Mrs. Daly says. "I hope not."

"But we did hate you. Danny slashed your tires. Mom made crank calls. She wanted to scare you away. I even helped."

"Are you all right now?"

"Am *I* all right? I threw rocks at your house. At your *dog*, Mrs. Daly."

I hide my face.

"I'm sorry," I say. "So sorry."

"You take things hard," Mrs. Daly says.

"I was bad. Really bad. Even you say it—some things can't be fixed."

She touches my shoulder. Feather-light and gone.

"I meant to say, these things are not fixable by *you*. Not you, Angelyn."

"Who'll fix them? My mom, you mean?" I laugh—I can't help it.

"She was hard on you," Mrs. Daly says after a time.

I look up. "You didn't like Mom, did you?"

She fusses with her wrap. "I didn't care for her, no."

"The cops kept asking if anything happened between Danny and me. The lady asked too, over and over. Mrs. Daly, my mother never asked."

"I would have asked, if it were me."

"I know," I say.

"I could have done more." Her voice shakes.

"No," I say, turning. "You were great. You were—"

"I cared for you, Angelyn. Does it help to know I cared?"

I hold on her. "Yes. It does help."

"Tell me about you," Mrs. Daly says. "Tell me about school."

I talk. Jeni comes over. Cross-legged on the lawn, she listens.

Time passes like nothing.

A door opens at the back of the building. A woman's voice:

"Jeni! Time for lunch setup."

"Five minutes, Mom," she calls.

Jeni's mom crosses to us. She's taller than Jeni, thin like her.

"I'll bet you're Angelyn," she says. "I'm Kim."

Off-balance, I say hi. "How did you know me?"

She nods to Jeni. "This one talks about you."

Jeni flushes. "Not that much."

Her mom rubs Mrs. Daly's shoulder. "Eleanor talks about you too."

"She does?" Something settles in me.

"Mom, we'll bring Mrs. Daly around front," Jeni says.

We take the path slowly.

"Does Nathan come to see her a lot?" I ask.

"Every lunch," Jeni says. "Even on school days."

"Oh. Well, I don't want to see him."

"Did you guys—fight, or something?"

I look at her. "What did he say?"

"Just that he dropped you somewhere last night. Someplace he didn't know. He was pretty pissed, for Nathan."

I focus on Mrs. Daly's white curls. "Maybe now he'll leave me alone." Adding: "I'm glad she has him."

Jeni says, "I've been thinking about what happened at the frosty."

"I don't want to talk about that." Sharp with her.

"I'm going to say it. There's something wrong with that teacher. You should stay away from him."

"Don't talk about him. I mean it."

We turn the corner to the rose path. I stop.

"Give us a minute, all right?"

Jeni walks on. I kneel by Mrs. Daly.

"I liked seeing you so much," I say.

She puts out her hand. I take it. Hold her fingers carefully.

"I loved seeing you," Mrs. Daly says.

"I'll come back," I say. Eyes down.

"Will you, Angelyn?"

"I will," I say. *I'll try*, I think.

Jeni waits at the lobby door. Mrs. Daly smiles up at me.

"You're a wonderful girl," she says.

My eyes fill. "I will come back."

I'm light across the parking lot. Wanting to tell.

Mr. Rossi has the seat back. His head back.

"It was great," I say, climbing in. "Mrs. Daly is so cool. *Still* cool."

He's blinking, sitting up. "Good. Great."

"Mr. Rossi, I couldn't have done it without you. I wouldn't have!"

"All right, Angelyn. Now, you are going to have to guide me the rest of the way to your house."

I sit there. *That's it?*

"Thank you," I say.

He rubs his eyes. "Yeah, no problem."

"No, really," I say. "*Thank you*, Mr. Rossi." And stretch to hug him.

"Whoa!" he says, but there I am, against him.

Arms at his sides, he sighs. "Angelyn."

I breathe with him, our clean soap smell the same.

Hands at my elbows. "Enough, now."

I tuck my head under his chin. "I'm thanking you."

"You're like a *cat*," Mr. Rossi says. "A child."

I draw back. Face to face. I kiss him, a real kiss.

His lips are warm. Dry. Pulling from mine.

Mr. Rossi turns his head. I slide off.

"I'm not a cat," I say. "Not a child. Not to you."

"How far is your house?" He speaks coldly.

"About three miles. Why?"

"Is it walkable?" Mr. Rossi asks.

"Why would we walk it?" I ask. Shivering inside.

"I'm letting you off here," he says.

"Why? Don't be mad. What did I do?"

"You can't *be* that way with me, Angelyn. You can't do those things."

"I know. Okay." I'd say anything.

"Who is that?" Mr. Rossi asks.

I look.

Jeni stands at the nursing home gate. Alone. Watching.

"That's the girl from the frosty," he says. "Your friend from class."

"She's not my friend."

"Put on your seat belt," Mr. Rossi says.

Someone's egged my house. Slime trails on the door. Shells on the steps.

Mr. Rossi and I look from his car.

"Everything has to be right for me to see my son," he says.

"I know," I say.

"That girl could tell anyone. Anything."

"Jeni doesn't talk to anyone but me."

"This weekend was a disaster," he says.

I chew a knuckle. "Don't let her ruin it, Mr. Rossi."

"Don't let her ruin it?" he says, looking at me.

My stomach twists. "Okay, Jeni shouldn't have seen, but—"

"Angelyn, get out of the car, please."

I face the house. The mess I'll have to clean.

"I don't want to get out."

A pause. "Do you know who egged it?" Mr. Rossi asks.

STEVE. "I think so. Yeah."

He waits again. "Are you going to be okay here?"

I shut my eyes. "Can I stay with you tonight?"

"What?"

"It's not crazy." I talk fast. "Mom and him won't be back until tomorrow. Jeni—I'll talk to her on Monday. I already told her, *Back off.*"

"You can't stay with me," Mr. Rossi says. "I'm not running through the same arguments I used last night."

"You remember them?" I say. Then: "Sorry. But you can't get into any *more* trouble if I stay another night."

His mouth twitches. "Sure I could."

"What do you mean?"

"I think you know."

"But—tonight would be so much better. It would have to be."

Mr. Rossi looks up. "How's that?"

"You're not drunk. I'm not sad, stressed, or sweated-out."

"Not following," he says roughly.

"We could help each other," I say.

"Help each other do what?"

"Well." Shy with him, suddenly. "The thing is, I don't like sex. Sometimes touching feels good, but it never feels right. With you, I'm thinking—everything could work. Because you see more to me than anyone I've been with."

"Anyone you've been with?" Mr. Rossi swears softly. "Angelyn, who do you think I am?"

"Someone who—likes me." I'm sputtering. "Why are you making me say it? Why are you *pretending*?"

"Pretending. What am I pretending?"

"You've liked me all along. I know it. I *saw* you! I saw you look at me—" I touch my chest. *"Here."*

"At the frosty. Okay." Mr. Rossi nods. "Yes, I looked. Didn't mean to, didn't *want* to. I kicked myself after. Your shirt was tight, and you're—"

"What?" I ask, lasering in.

"Very pretty. You're very pretty, Angelyn."

"Thanks." Eyeing him.

"But there's a difference—a world's difference—between *looking* and doing anything about it. Or wanting to. Come on! I would never want you like that."

"Why?" I ask. Hurt. Not believing it.

"Because you're a child." Mr. Rossi is calmer. "You are a child, to me."

I feel myself losing. I put my hand between us on the gearshift.

"I'll prove to you I'm not."

He stares at the hand. "I'm not who you're looking for."

"You are," I say. "You are exactly. I would never tell. No one would know."

"I'd know," he says. "You'd know. That would be enough."

"Yes," I say. "That would be enough."

Mr. Rossi curls his hand over mine. I breathe in sharply.

Lifting it, he sets it on my lap.

"What you're saying is wrong. Dead wrong. Don't you know that?"

"Who says?" I ask. Flattened.

"Everyone says it, Angelyn. Everybody does."

"They're not here." I remember something. "I'm the prettiest girl of the day. Today."

"What?" Mr. Rossi looks over.

"You said that at the frosty. *'The prettiest girl of the day.'*"

"I didn't mean you. I didn't. I was miles away."

"Oh." I try to smile. "I'm at least as cute as Dolly. Take me home, Mr. Rossi. Take me anyway."

He holds the wheel. "Get out of the car."

"I don't understand. My boyfriend said, *Leave*, because I wouldn't do it all, and you—Mr. Rossi, I'd do anything for you!"

"Out, now."

"But I *like* you." I'm fumbling for the door handle. "I like you too."

"Sweetheart, get out."

I look at him sharply. And crawl out.

CHAPTER TWENTY-TWO

With garden gloves I grab eggshells by the handful. I hose the door, the steps, and scrub them down. I clean inside—the dishes, the beds, the sweeping, the dusting. Anything to move.

Not good enough for him.

I've got the TV on blasting *stuff* about *stuff.* Anytime I stop, it's like I've run ten miles.

Not good.

Dark comes. I pull a smoke from a pack Mom's hid and have it outside. On the porch steps I stare across to a house that looks like ours. It's empty—up for rent for months. At Mrs. Daly's old place next door, someone's cooking meat. Another rental, where no one stays for long.

A truck blasts by. It comes around again, slower.

"Hey, honey," the driver calls. He's older, mustached, features in shadow.

He would.

"No," I say, and straighten. "No," I say, and go inside.

Room to room, I lock what can be locked. Back in front, I stare at the heavy mustard drape that hides the outside.

I can feel him there. See his truck parked.

Rushing to the window, I pull the drape aside—

and JUMP at my own reflection.

My hair's a wild cloud. My eyes, panic-wide. My mouth, an open wound.

The street is empty.

He would've. If he could.

I turn from the window.

Danny would have—if he'd had the chance.

My hands shake. I don't know what to do.

Homework, I think, and it's like an oasis.

Then I remember.

My homework's with her.

Sunday they're back late, scrabbling at the lock, stumbling laughing into the house. I'm in bed, covers to my chin, dressed underneath.

Mom calls and my eyes snap shut.

She comes in my room. "You best behaved yourself."

I imitate a corpse.

"She's here, at least," Mom says.

When they're quiet an hour, I slip outside.

I check the truck. Twice, like I could miss it.

The backpack isn't there.

In their doorway I shout: "WHERE IS IT?"

Mom sits up. "Angelyn?" Her nightie is rumpled, and I see too much.

I fix on a point above her. "Where's the backpack?"

"Wait," she says a couple of times. Then: "What?"

"You drove off with it. My homework!"

Danny lifts his head. "What's this now?"

Looking at him, I lose what I want to say next.

Rubbing on himself, Nathan said. *Making faces.*

His chest is saggy. Not solid like before. Chest hair's turned
to gray.

I tell him: "You're disgusting."

I whisper it.

Mom looks between us. "Save it for the morning."

I shake my head. "I don't care about *him.* I need my stuff NOW."

She shrugs a sleeve in place. "You are way out of line."

"I want to do my homework. Is that out of line?"

Mom laughs. "Your homework?"

I step in. "This is serious. This is real."

She fires me with hard eyes. "You better stop."

Danny says, "Get out of our room."

"Shut up," I say. And *scream* it. "Asshole! Shut up shut up
shut up."

Mom's flipping covers. "*Run* to your bed."

Danny is sinking. Flat on the mattress, hands up like I've got
a gun.

Like *I* do.

Mom drives me to school. Shut tight, I face the side.

She turns by the auditorium. "You want to be left here, right?"

I make a sound that could be "Yes."

She pulls over. "I didn't take your backpack on purpose."

I look at her.

"We didn't know we had it. Not until the first coffee stop."

"Where is it?" My voice is rusty.

"Still in Sacramento," Mom says.

"You left the backpack."

"No. I forgot it. At the motel. We'll get it back."

"When? I'm already missing assignments."

"I go for training again this weekend. We'll get it then."

"The weekend! Mom, I need the books now."

"I can't just pick up and go in a workweek. You know that."

"What am I supposed to do without my stuff?"

"Borrow. Explain to your teachers. I'll write you a note.
Whatever!"

I nod to myself. "Okay, then."

"Angelyn, I know your schoolwork is important. I'm sorry."

Sorry? Mom never is.

I stand in the breezeway, cold.

"Angelyn!" Steve's voice.

From the pool area. He's running.

Flutter of fear. I stand tall and still.

Steve skids to a stop. "What the hell?"

I lift my chin. "You tell me. What the hell?"

"Friday night! I came back and you were gone."

"You egged my house. I knew it was you."

"I egged it—*yeah.* I was pissed! Angelyn, where did you go?"

"What do you care? Why did you even come back? Just for that?"

"No," Steve says. "That was after. I waited for you. I waited an hour!"

"What for?" I ask.

"I thought—" He stops. "I thought maybe I shouldn't have left that way."

"I told you to go."

"Yeah, but—" Steve checks me. "Something was going on before that."

I look away. "Don't get complicated. You came back for another shot."

"No—hey, Angelyn, you called *me*. You said we were going to happen."

"I didn't say that. You thought that."

Steve flips his hands. "Okay, so why'd you ask me over?"

I swallow past a lump. "Because I was lonely."

"Oh man."

"It's the truth."

"Maybe this is too much for me," Steve says.

"You think?"

"What do you want, Angelyn? I'm asking serious."

I wilt. Steve looks pretty deflated too.

"I have no clue."

"You are messed up," he says. Like: *You have brown eyes.*

Lips pressed, I nod. "Why do you keep coming back?"

He looks me in the eye. Looks lower.

"Oh, these." I sweep hands over my breasts, my hips.

"Yeah, those." He's pissed again. "And, I like you. Sometimes."

"I don't like how you like me."

Steve sighs. "You mess *me* up."

"Leave, then, and leave me alone."

He looks off. "I saw you with your mom. You guys okay?"

"Well, she stole my backpack, but . . ."

"I know. I saw. I was there."

"Now she's saying—just more crap."

Steve flexes like a wrestler. "That bitch. Let's steal it back."

I laugh. His face softens.

"Man, you keep me guessing."

"Is that good or bad?"

Steve tilts his head. "Come here and find out."

I bite my lip. "No."

He comes to me. Arms around, rocking.

"Steve." I don't help him or stop him.

"Why do we fight?" he asks. "I never want to fight."

"I have to go," I say, my hands on his arms.

"I'll walk you," Steve says.

He slings an arm around, keeping it anchored.

"Come to the street, Angelyn. Everyone wants to see you."

I glance at him. "I'm sure. Anyway, I don't want to see them."

Steve points to the Humanities Building. "You'd rather be with her?"

Jeni is above, watching from the second-floor corridor.

"Creep," I say.

He lifts his arm, laughing. "See you."

I climb the stairs. Jeni waits for me at the top.

"Hi," she says like she's taking my temperature.

I shoulder past.

She follows me to the rail. "Are you back with him?"

"Am I *here* or with him?" I say.

"You're here. But I wondered."

"Stop wondering."

Jeni stands back. "Mrs. Daly was so happy you came."

I smile a little. "Good."

"She told Nathan you were there."

My fingers close on the rail. "Uh-huh."

"Angelyn—" Jeni stops.

I look over. "Go ahead."

"All right. I saw you in the parking lot with that teacher."

"I know you did. So what?"

"*Kissing,*" she says, widening her eyes.

"It wasn't *kissing,*" I say, dramatic like her. "Turned out to be—nothing."

"That's where Nathan dropped you. His place. You spent the night with him."

I look out on the field. "You don't know what you're talking about."

"Angelyn, it's wrong."

"So everyone says."

"Yeah, but do you *get* it?"

"You know, not a great day for a lecture."

"I don't mean to lecture—but sleeping with some older guy, some teacher? That's not you. It doesn't have to be."

I let go of the rail. "You can stop there."

Jeni powers on. "Whatever happened at your house—"

"My stepdad stuck his hands down my pants," I say. "Nine million times."

She's stopped. Mouth open.

"It's different hearing it from me, huh?" I catch my breath. "Instead of Nathan."

"I'm sorry," Jeni says.

I warn her with a look. "Don't be. And don't think you know me."

"So—your stepfather messed you over. Now Mr. Rossi—"

I dip for my backpack and remember it's not there. "You're wrong about him. Still wrong."

Jeni searches me. "Well, what's right?"

"I didn't have sex with Mr. Rossi. Because *he* wouldn't."

She stares like she's not hearing right.

"Yeah," I say. "*I* asked, and Mr. Rossi said no."

"Oh," Jeni says.

"Or don't you believe me?"

"If you say so, I do." She's frowning.

"It's true." I turn my head. "I am that freak."

"You're not a freak."

"I'm going to wait somewhere else," I say.

Jeni walks into my sight line. "Don't go."

I look at her carefully. "Are you blocking me?"

"No. Angelyn, listen. I've got something to tell you."

"What?"

Her face crumples.

"What?" Scared now.

"It's hard," Jeni says, head down.

I wipe my hands on my jeans. "Say it."

Above us, the intercom crackles to life.

"Angelyn Stark to the office, please. Angelyn Stark."

I stare at it and down to her. "Oh, you did not."

She looks up. Tears.

"Jeni, you *told*? You told already?"

She wipes her eyes. "No—"

"Mr. Rossi will hate me." I'm dizzy. "Oh my God, his *son*."

"His son?"

"What about my *mom*? I'll never get my backpack now."

"You're not making sense," Jeni says.

"I'll be blamed. I'll get blamed again."

"Angelyn, stop!"

I'm walking at her. "You stop. Messing in my life."

Jeni puts up her hands. "You can explain."

I stop.

"You can tell them the truth," she says.

I look at her blankly.

"I'm trying to be a friend, Angelyn. I'm trying to be your friend."

"We're done," I say. Cold, not hot.

CHAPTER TWENTY-THREE

The vice principal's office. Miss Bass is at her desk. Mr. Rossi stands against the wall. From a visitor's chair, Mom is looking like she's already judged me and hanged me.

I turn out my hands. "What?"

Mom leans in. "His *house*, Angelyn?"

I lean away. "Nobody died."

"That's not what I'm asking."

"Why did you go there?" Miss Bass asks.

I circle a toe on the blond carpet. "No reason."

Mom snorts. "Can't leave town without a major crisis."

"You left her alone, Sherry?" Miss Bass says.

"A day," Mom says. "Two. She's not a baby."

"No. But Angelyn is in need of supervision."

"She'll get that, Miss Bass. Don't worry."

I look to Mr. Rossi. He turns to Miss Bass.

"Do I really need to be here?"

"Yes," she says. "We all do."

"It was my idea."

Everyone looks at me.

"My dumb idea," I add. "Mr. Rossi didn't know."

"What am I hearing?" Mom says. "You're taking responsibility?"

I sit straight. "Give me the punishment, Miss Bass."

"This happened off school grounds," she says. "I don't have a punishment for you, Angelyn. I'm still concerned."

"So am I." Mom is staring at me. "All right. Tell us what you did."

What did Jeni say I did?

"Whatever happened, it was all me."

"Now, just a minute," Mr. Rossi says. "Angelyn showed up at my house uninvited, and that's all there is to it."

Okay. No Mrs. Daly, no kiss, no—

"She spent the night," Mom says.

Mr. Rossi says, "Yes."

"He didn't do anything wrong!" I say. "He wants his son to be all right."

Mom says, "What?"

Miss Bass says, "I don't understand."

Mr. Rossi: "Angelyn, would you just *be quiet.*"

I've got my mouth covered. Too late.

"Some—personal issues came up while she was there," Mr. Rossi says.

"What personal issues?" Mom's face is red.

I sink in the chair. "Mr. Rossi means *his* stuff. Not mine."

"Uh-huh. And who slept where?"

"Mom!"

"Angelyn slept outside," Mr. Rossi says.

"On the porch," I add.

"What the—*hell*—is this?" Mom asks.

Miss Bass clears her throat. "Folks, let's take a moment."

I can hear Mom breathing.

"Angelyn, how did you find Mr. Rossi's house?" Miss Bass says.

All I can see is Dolly there, that first time.

Mr. Rossi's face reads: *scared.*

"I looked it up in Mom's school directory," I say.

"You went in my personal things?" Mom says. "You are such a sneak."

I swallow. "Okay."

"And a liar. She never mentioned this."

Mr. Rossi stands from the wall. "I'd say Angelyn is confused."

Confused?

Miss Bass checks him. "How do you mean, Mr. Rossi?"

Mom says, "Yeah. I want to hear this."

"She's got me down as some kind of father figure," Mr. Rossi says.

"I do not!"

He looks at me a second. "Or—as something more than that."

"*What* more?" Mom asks.

"We're friends," I say tightly. "Nothing but friends."

"I don't think Angelyn knows the difference," Mr. Rossi says.

"What difference?" Mom asks.

"Friend. Father. Lover. She's got the lines blurred."

"He can't say that." Mom looks at Miss Bass. "He can't say those things!"

I'm staring at my lap.

"*Student* is all Angelyn should be to you, Mr. Rossi," Miss Bass says.

"I'm aware of that."

"Wait a minute!" Mom is loud. "Angelyn isn't 'confused.' She's done this before."

I look at her. "I've never gone to a teacher's house before."

Mom's face is set. "When Angelyn was twelve years old—"

I stop breathing.

She blinks. "No, thirteen. When Angelyn was thirteen, she and a friend left a party and snuck into a neighbor's yard with two older boys to use the hot tub."

I can't believe her. "Mom! That was a long time ago."

"You haven't changed! Not with this stunt."

"I'm not sure how this is relevant," Miss Bass says.

"There's more," Mom says. "The neighbors spotted the kids. They almost called the police. That would have been perfect. Angelyn was drunk out of her mind. They all were. The boys were seventeen—eighteen. All naked."

"Don't *tell* them that." My voice cracks.

Mom glances at me. "*This* is Angelyn. Not confused. This is how she is."

Struck speechless, I can't raise my eyes. The silence goes on.

"Mr. Rossi," Miss Bass says, "how do you feel about Angelyn remaining in your class?"

I peek at Mr. Rossi. He's staring at Mom.

"It's my best class." I force the words.

"Where would she go instead?" Mom says, shifting.

"We want a solution that fits everyone," Miss Bass says.

"Dumping her out of class is no solution," Mom says. "How would she make up the credit?"

"We're into second quarter," Mr. Rossi says. "It would be tough. I guess she'd have to retake at some point."

"Mr. Rossi, please." I try to think. "I won't go to your house again. I promise."

"Angelyn has to know there are lines you do not cross." He's saying it to me.

"I do know that!" I say. "Really. I do."

"I'll keep my foot on her," Mom says. "Count on it. And you, Mr. Rossi—you keep your distance."

Miss Bass looks at him. "Well?"

Mr. Rossi waits. "I'm okay with Angelyn in class."

Miss Bass nods. She thanks us. Bruised, I stand with Mom.

Miss Bass tells Mr. Rossi to stay.

Outside, Mom throws me questions and directions. I don't listen.

My first two classes don't register. All I can think about is seeing him.

Mr. Rossi is behind his newspaper when I come in.

I walk to his desk. "Are you okay?"

He lowers the paper an inch. "Angelyn, take your seat."

Jeni isn't here yet. About ten kids in the room.

"I want to change seats. Is that all right?"

"Sit down." Mr. Rossi's voice is firm and final.

Shakily, I sit.

Jacey and Charity walk in. Jacey catches my eye and smiles.

Nerves pinballing, I look away.

One row over, people talk about Homecoming. I can't tell if it's already happened or hasn't yet. Someone mentions a reality show, and everybody laughs. I jerk at the sound and hope no one has seen.

In singles, pairs, and bunches, kids roll into class. None of them are Jeni.

"Mr. Rossi! I don't want to sit here anymore. Not by *her*."

His newspaper crackles. He flips a page.

I point across to the first row, the second desk empty all year. "Can I sit there?"

The paper stays in place, Mr. Rossi's fingers pulling it taut.

Jacey waves. "Angelyn!" She points to my old desk in front of Charity.

"I don't think so," I say.

Everyone is listening. Watching. Everyone but him.

"Come back to us," Jacey says. "We want you with us. Don't we, Charity?"

Charity thumps a boot against the book rack on my desk. "Yeah. We do."

She doesn't mean it.

I look at Jeni's empty desk and the row across the room lined with kids I never talk to.

"All right," I say to Jacey. To Charity. I feel my mouth turn down.

Charity leans up as I slide in. "You're fighting with that girl?"

"Yeah," I say. "Hate her."

"Awesome! Why?"

"Because she's a fucking snitch." I say it clearly.

Mr. Rossi lowers the newspaper. He stares at me.

The bell rings.

"Get out your homework," he says.

"I *couldn't* do it," I say by his desk. "I didn't have a book."

Mr. Rossi erases the board. "No homework, you take a zero."

The door shuts behind the last one out. We're alone.

"You saw how I was this weekend. My mom took all my school stuff."

Mr. Rossi walks to the door and props it open.

"I gave you my answer," he says.

"I still don't have my book. Will you loan me one so I can keep up?"

He keeps a hand on the door. "Share with a friend."

"I don't have friends in this class." My voice is hard.

"I can't help you," Mr. Rossi says.

I point to the bookcase by the board. "I see some extras there."

"Stop it," he says.

"Mr. Rossi, you're acting like you're mad at me."

A shake of his head, he looks to the hallway.

"Is it—" I swallow. "Is it because of what my mom said about me?"

Mr. Rossi looks back to me. "No, Angelyn."

"Okay." I breathe out. "I'm not pissed at you. I know you had to say those things about me in Miss B's office."

"I meant them," Mr. Rossi says.

"You were covering up."

"I was not covering up."

"We covered for each other," I say.

He checks outside again. "We can't talk like this. We can't talk at all."

"I'm sorry I mentioned your son. I don't think they noticed much."

Mr. Rossi shuts his eyes. "I have to treat you like any student. You have to *be* like any student."

"I am like any student." I lean against his desk. "I want to be."

"If you don't do your homework, you take a zero. You lose a book, you find it or pay for it. I don't help you outside class. You're the student, I'm the teacher, and that's how we get along."

I blink through his speech. "Miss Bass told you to say all that."

"She warned me. She was right."

"Warned you. Like I'm—hazardous to your health or something."

"You are," Mr. Rossi says. "You could be. You know that. You're not dumb."

"Didn't I look out for you in there? Didn't I *not* say anything about Dolly? She's a secret between us and I kept it!"

"That's enough." He's so quiet.

"You were right about Jeni." I force a laugh. "I told her off. I scared her out of class today."

"Did you mean anything you said in that office? About how things were your fault, and they wouldn't happen again?"

"My fault," I say slowly. "I won't go to your house again. But we can still talk. Can't we? We're still friends."

"I don't know how many ways to say this, Angelyn. Stay away from me."

"Oh." I'm standing.

"For both of us," he says. "I could lose my *job*. Do you want to be pulled from this class?"

I make it to the door. "What did you keep me here for anyway?"

"Because you're a student," Mr. Rossi says. "You deserve another chance. Don't make me sorry I did."

A girl walks in. She walks between us. Glasses, blond hair.

He straightens. "Hey, Courtney. Angelyn, time to get going."

"The Coast Guard," I say. "What about that?"

"What about it?" he says in the tiredest voice ever.

"You said we'd talk about it. You promised, and it hasn't happened yet."

The girl is staring. She hasn't even sat.

"You can find that information on the Net," Mr. Rossi says.

Finally, I understand.

"Everything's over. Because Jeni couldn't keep her stupid mouth shut."

More people come in. I push through them.

Mr. Rossi doesn't call me back.

Steve's heart beats against my back. His legs curve around mine.

Charity sits at the other end of the truck. "Did Rossi change the grade?"

Our hands twine. "No," I say.

"He was treating you mean," she says.

Steve puts his face by mine. "What did Rossi do?"

"I needed a book and he wouldn't lend me one. He said, *Go buy it.*"

"Sounds like him. Charity, lend her yours."

Her face gets pink. "I don't have mine today."

"Sure you don't," I say. And tilt my head to Steve.

We kiss, scraping cheeks.

"Like we never stopped," he says.

I curl into him. "Yeah."

"I'll get that book for you," Steve says. "Jacey's got to have one."

"Never mind. I'm done working for Rossi."

He stands so fast his knee clunks my head.

"Ow!" I look up. "What are you doing?"

Sprawled across the cab, Steve shouts for JT and Jacey.

I pull up my knees and rub my head.

"He told us to let you back in," Charity says.

I make a face. Not surprised. Not really.

"You're so lucky. Everyone comes to you."

"Sitting here," I say, "you might see it different."

Charity looks at Steve. "No, I wouldn't."

Jacey and JT come to the truck. Steve asks about the book.

"Angelyn can *have* mine," Jacey says.

Steve squats beside me. "Problem solved."

I lift my lips. "Thanks."

"Yep," Charity says. "Angelyn always gets what she wants."

Steve nudges me. "Well, who wouldn't give it to her?"

"I know a couple of people," I say.

JT and Jacey pile in.

"The reservoir tomorrow for lunch?" JT says.

Steve says, "You know it."

I look around. "All of us?"

JT laughs in Charity's direction. "*She's* not comin'."

Jacey says, "*Aww,*" like he's kicked a puppy.

"What'd that girl snitch about, Angelyn?" Charity's voice is
ragged.

"What girl?" Steve asks.

"Nothing." I sit forward. "No one. I'm taking care of it."

"Wait, the one that was watching us this morning?"

"Angelyn's girlfriend," Charity says. "But they broke up."

"Shut up," I say.

"Why didn't she come to class?" Jacey asks. "I mean, if she
was here."

"She knew better than to come," I say.

Charity grins. "Did you break her heart, Angelyn?"

"Girl drama," Steve says when I don't answer that one.

JT stretches. "Never know what Angelyn's up to or who she's doing."

I look at him. "What?"

Jacey slaps his chest. "Be nice!"

JT catches her hand. "Just playing."

I turn to Steve. "That's okay with you?"

He shifts. "Hey, man—JT. C'mon."

I wait for more. Nothing comes.

"I'm not going to the reservoir with anyone but you," I say.

Steve smiles. "Sweet."

I face away.

He spiders his fingers on my back. "Hey."

"Don't," I say.

His fingers tickle. I roll my shoulders. Steve starts a massage.

The truck is like a rowboat, sunk with all of us.

"Hey, Angelyn," Charity says.

I screw my face shut. "I am not hearing it."

"Oh, but you'll want to hear this. Here comes your girlfriend."

CHAPTER TWENTY-FOUR

Jeni is coming through the auto yard, arm to her chest holding something.

"That is the girl from this morning," Steve says.

"Yeah." My cool cracks. I hold my head a moment.

Raising it: "You're crazy coming here!"

Jeni calls, "I've got some things for you."

I roll to my knees. "I don't want anything from you."

JT laughs. "Tell her, Angelyn."

"Run her off," Jacey says.

"Kick her ass," Charity says.

Steve is looking up at me.

Jeni marches on. I'm back at the office with everybody on me. Facing Mr. Rossi as he tells me: "Stay away."

She stops an arm's length from the truck.

"What are you *doing*?" I ask.

Jeni holds up a World Cultures text, her folder stuck inside.

"You're giving me your book? How did you know—"

Steve pops up beside me. "We've got the book situation covered."

"The notes for our report are here too," Jeni says. "You'll need them, Angelyn."

"Like you won't? Forget it, Jeni. I'm not doing the report. You do it. It's yours."

"I can't," she says. "We're moving. Like, now."

All I can think to say is, "Why?"

Jeni pulls her arm down. "Does it matter why? I tried to tell you this morning."

"This morning?"

She pushes the book at me again. The notes. "Take the stuff, all right? And turn my book in?"

I sit back. "Turn your book in? After you trash me and—"

"I didn't say *anything*." Jeni looks as mad as I've ever seen her. "I don't care if you don't believe me."

She's lying, I think. "You're lying."

"Yeah," Charity says. "Angelyn hates you. Snitch."

Jeni's face twitches.

I look around. "Hey, I've got this!"

The girls and JT smirk at me.

Steve asks what's going on.

My head droops. "I don't know. All right?"

Charity says my name singsong. Pointing.

Jeni is walking away.

I look at Steve. "It's not over with her."

"Then go," he says. "And, Angelyn? Come back."

■ ■ ■

I stand with Jeni in the auto yard among wrecked cars and rusted parts.

"Did you come to kick my ass?" she says. Little and fierce. "You won't have it around much longer."

I check the truck. They're hanging off it. "Are you trying to show me up, coming here?"

"No." Jeni pulls the book to her chest. "I really did want to give you the World Cultures stuff."

"Right." I kick the nubby asphalt. "The office was rough. Mr. Rossi was there. My mom too. And Miss Bass. They were all over me for going to his house."

194

"You weren't in that office because of me, Angelyn."

I look at her.

"Do you really think—" Jeni stops. "Really think I'd go find that lady before school and tell her how you spent your weekend?"

"Not the weekend," I say faintly. "Just one night."

"Who else knew you went there?"

"Nathan. But he didn't know whose place it was. Unless you told him."

Jeni says, "I didn't tell anyone! So, not Nathan. Who else?"

I get it. "Oh no. Mr. Rossi didn't tell. Why would he?"

"Maybe so he wouldn't get in worse trouble?"

"That doesn't make sense," I say.

"He's a teacher. He's an adult. They do what they have to, to keep going."

"But—Miss Bass said he could dump me from his class. Mr. Rossi said I could stay."

Jeni shrugs.

"If he were mad at me—if he *told*—why would he give me another chance?"

"I don't know." She pushes the book into my hands. "Take this, all right?"

I hold it loosely. The folder slips. "I'm not doing the report. I meant that."

"You should. We put in the work."

"Hey, Angelyn!"

We both look. Steve is standing in the truck. He waves.

"Well," Jeni says.

"Listen," I say. "I believe you. I don't know that Mr. Rossi told, but I believe you didn't."

Her face smooths. "Okay."

"Really?"

Jeni points over her shoulder. "Walk me out?"

We pick our way around the oil spots.

"It took guts to come here," I say.

"You scared me this morning."

"I know."

"I don't like being scared. I *won't* be scared. That's why I came back."

I nod. "You knew where to find me."

"I checked the library first," she says.

I laugh, then Jeni does. "So, why are you moving?"

"Mom's *romance* ended, and we have to leave town."

"Oh."

"That's how things work out for her. They *never* work out for her."

"Where are you guys going to go?" I ask.

"Back to San Jose. Mom has a friend who lets us crash. Nathan's taking us to catch the train."

I walk slower. Down the steps out of the auto yard, I see Nathan's truck parked on the street.

Jeni stops. "I'm sick of it, Angelyn."

I don't know what to say.

"My life won't be like hers. I have to believe it."

"It's up to us, right?" My words sound hollow.

"Things are always ending," Jeni says.

"You'll make things happen. What you want to have happen."

She looks at me. "How can you know that?"

I pull up words like water from a well. "The way you've been with me."

"Okay," Jeni says, "then I'll tell you this—don't give up on Rossi's class."

"It's going to suck, being there. He can hardly look at me."

"It's not about him. Get the grades for you. Do it for you."

I dip my head. "It'll sound crazy, but I wish you weren't leaving."

"I wish that too," Jeni says.

I lose hold of the book. It hits the ground and the folder slides, spilling pages.

Jeni and I crouch at the same time. She reaches the papers first and hands them to me. I thank her and stick them in the folder.

We stand together.

With a tiny smile, she says, "Guess you *really* don't want to do the report."

I tuck the book and folder to my chest and make a show of holding them.

Jeni looks toward Nathan's truck. "Anyway—"

"You would have believed me," I say.

She turns.

"I told Jacey about my stepdad. Back in seventh grade. It was during this health assembly. You know, some lady saying we shouldn't let boys touch our private parts. We were being little bitches, asking if anyone had ever touched hers. We got sent out and ran and hid in the bathroom. So, we're fixing our hair, and I say: *'My stepdad touches me.'*"

"That must have been so hard," Jeni says.

"No. It slipped out. I didn't plan it. Anyway, Jacey laughed."

"She did? Wow."

"*'Oh, Angelyn, he does not.'*" I say it from memory.

"Maybe that's all she had in her," Jeni says.

"Maybe. She never told Charity. That was all I cared about."

"You're right," Jeni says. "I would have believed you."

Down the walkway: "Before all that this morning," Jeni says, "I was going to ask—do you want to write back and forth?"

"Write?"

She looks sideways. "Letters. You know, not texting."

"I know what they are. But I don't really write."

"Okay." She says it fast.

"My mom would be all up on me if I started getting mail. You know."

"Sure," Jeni says. "It's just—maybe we weren't ever really friends, but this is the first time it mattered. To me."

I think of something. "If you wrote care of Mrs. Daly, I could get the letters then."

Her smile lights her face. "I'll do that."

Their things are in the bed of Nathan's truck. A duffel. Two shabby suitcases. Jeni's backpack. Her mom is in the cab next to Nathan. Rumpled. Tearstruck.

"We'll miss the train!" she says.

Jeni looks at me. "I know, Mom."

I nod to her. "You take care."

"You too, Angelyn."

Nathan starts the truck.

"Wait." I cross in front. "Hey."

He stares ahead.

I curl my fingers on the window ledge. "I talked to your grandma."

"Yeah. Thanks."

"We talked about—what you and me talked about."

Nathan's jaw works. "Uh-huh."

"So now you don't care."

"Thought you didn't want me to care, Angelyn."

I shift. "I got into big old trouble, going to that place you took me."

Good, I hear him think.

"Someone I thought wanted me—didn't want me at all."

"So what?" Nathan says, but now he's looking at me.

"So—that makes me sad, like you."

He snorts.

"*Sad*," I say. "Like you."

Nathan glances at Jeni and her mom. "I shouldn't have kissed you."

"I shouldn't have kissed you," I say.

He winces.

"I mean—Nathan, find someone you like who can like you. You shouldn't have to figure me out."

"I'm not even going to try, Angelyn. Not anymore."

"What are you going to do after you drop out?" I ask.

"I'm going to work," he says. "I'm good at working."

"That's cool," I say, and Nathan looks at me again.

Jeni leans across her mom. "Guys, we really do have to go."

Nathan clears his throat. "Yeah, we're leaving."

I let the ledge go. "I don't hate you."

His shoulders straighten.

"All right?"

"I heard you," Nathan says.

I can't tell if it matters to him or not.

"It's— It's good you stopped him," I say.

Nathan looks at me. "What?"

"You heard."

He waits. "I never thought I'd hear that."

"Yeah, well." Hardest of all, I say it: "Thanks."

Nathan fights a smile and lets it through. "Sure, Angelyn."

I stumble crossing back, a hand to the hood to catch me.

Jeni mouths, *Bye*, as they pull away. I nod from the sidewalk.

Goodbye.

200 "Friend, father, *lover*." Mom spits the last word. "What was *that*?"

I'm slumped, stuck beside her as we inch through town traffic.

"Let's don't talk about it," I say.

"We're talking about it."

Someone honks.

"I think you're supposed to move," I say.

Mom punches into the intersection.

"What have you been saying to that teacher?"

"Nothing, Mom. I told him nothing. So—nothing to worry about."

I rest my head against the window. It bumps gently as we move. Air from the vent cools my face, and the sun warms my hair. I close my eyes and drift into something like sleep, knowing every turn, stop, and merge as Mom makes it.

Close to home, she takes the turn hard off the highway. My shoulder rolls. My head knocks against the window.

"What?" I ask, pulling myself up.

She speeds along our route, dug in with her shoulders.

"Mom?"

Hard again, she swerves from the road, the truck's wheels spinning into a stretch of gravel and weeds.

I grip the seat. "Mom!"

The truck tilts as we run along a ditch, a cow pasture on the other side.

"What's wrong?" I shout. With a jump she lifts her foot from gas to brake.

The truck jolts to a stop at the rise of an asphalted path into the pasture.

Bent at the wheel, Mom looks at me. "You've been talking about our family."

"I have *not.*"

"Then how would he know to say that?"

I straighten. "How would *who* know to say—*what?*"

"Him! Mr. Rossi. 'Friend, father, lover.' You tell me what that means."

"He said I had the lines blurred." I'm embarrassed, remembering.

"Either you've been talking with that man or you've had some kind of *relations* with him."

"Relations?" I feel sick. And glad that Mr. Rossi told me no.

Mom juts her chin. "Well?"

I'll say it. "Everyone isn't like Danny."

She punch-pulls my shoulder. "You stop with that!"

I wrench from her. "Don't touch me!"

I'm in the weeds, shaking.

The air is hot and still.

Mom comes after.

"You are going to lose me that job. What'll Miss Bass think of me now?"

"I don't care about your job!"

She *runs* at me. Mom doesn't run. I face her, blinking hair out of my eyes.

"I've got just as much reason to be pissed as you. Why did you say that *crap* about me to Miss Bass and Mr. Rossi? They liked me, and now—"

Mom laughs, more of a bark. "*He* likes you, all right!"

I stare at her. "I think we should forget this. I will if you will."

Her eyes narrow. "What did you tell Mr. Rossi?"

"*Nothing.*"

"Oh, it's something. The way he looked at you."

"Mr. Rossi didn't look at me. He looked anywhere else."

"The way he didn't look, then. Like he was *scared* to look."

"Danny's scared to look," I say.

Hands on hips. "Danny, again."

"He's scared to look. Do we really want to go there, Mom? Do you?"

She studies me. "Are you confused, Angelyn, like your teacher said?"

"Yeah. I'm confused." Totally sarcastic.

A muscle car zips past, a *vroom* from nowhere and gone.

I sweep a hand to the road. "Can we go? I want to go."

Mom nods. "I'm bringing Danny in on this."

"No!" I call after her. "Hey! I've got *more* reason to be pissed than you."

She keeps on toward the truck. I follow, nowhere else to go.

CHAPTER TWENTY-FIVE

Danny's in the hall when we come in. A towel tucked in his pants.

He thumbs to the kitchen. "Hey, Sherry, I made dinner."

Mom shakes her head. "We've got to talk."

"Something wrong?" he asks.

I stand between them. "I have to go to the bathroom."

"So, go," Mom says.

When I come back, they're in the front room. Danny's in the armchair and Mom is on the couch. She slaps a spot beside her.

"No," I say, standing at the wall.

"We're doing this," Mom says.

"I'm tired and I don't feel right. I need to lie down."

"You know something, Angelyn? I'm tired and I don't feel right either. Come here and lie down if you want to lie down."

"No," I say. "Not there."

Mom says, "Why not?"

I make my mouth tight.

Mom nods to Danny. "Say something to her."

"Act right," he tells me. "It's past time."

Head down, I fold my arms.

"Let's do this in the kitchen," he says.

Danny's made tacos. He takes his time setting them up. My gut is like iron.

Mom taps the table. "What's the occasion?"

"I picked up a job today," Danny says over his shoulder. "A lady wants me to install new gutters. If she likes the work, she's got more that needs doing."

"You're getting paid up front?"

"Half now, half when the job is done. Same as always."

Mom grunts. "It's been so long I've forgot."

Danny sets the platter on the table and sits beside her.

"Sherry, what's going on?" he says.

The tacos look foul, flopped in a slab, grease weeping through the sides. Pooling on the plate. The spice smell gets up my nose.

"Angelyn was in trouble today at school," Mom says.

"That's not new," Danny says.

"This kind of trouble is."

"What'd she do now?" he asks.

"While we were out of town," Mom says, "Angelyn spent the night at a teacher's house. A *male* teacher's house."

Danny takes a couple of tacos. "That's deep."

"Shut up," I say. Under my breath.

"We had a little meeting about it," Mom says after a pause. "The vice principal, the teacher, Angelyn, and me."

Danny crunches. "Is the guy in trouble?"

The question hangs. Mom doesn't answer it. She looks at me.

My heart beats faster. "Mr. Rossi shouldn't be in trouble."

Sour-faced, Danny chews on.

"*He* shouldn't be," I add.

Danny swallows what he's got. "Sherry, you want to call her off?"

"You can look at her, Dan," Mom says.

"What?" he says. I'm frowning.

"Angelyn thinks you're scared to look at her."

"Don't *tell* him that," I say. Then: "He is scared. He is!"

Danny says: "Your mother told me not to."

"Mom, you did?" I ask, and we're quiet.

"Do you want to look at her?" Mom is hoarse.

"Hell no!" He's loud.

"That teacher picked up some funny ideas somewhere," Mom says.

Danny's looking at me now. "What are you stirring up?"

I search him. Dull brown eyes, and nothing reflected back.

"I'm not stirring up anything," I say. "People are seeing it in me."

What you put there.

"Am I being accused of something?" he says, staring now.

Mom nods to me. "This is Angelyn's show."

"It isn't," I say. "Mom, I don't know what you want."

"Sherry, she pushes herself at people," Danny says. "That's the problem."

I do not. The words catch in my mouth.

"She pushed herself at me." He waves in my direction. "Twelve years old, and built *almost* like that."

"Don't say how she's built." Mom is almost absent.

I lean in. To cover myself. To talk to him. "I didn't push. We were friends. You said so."

Danny's lip curls. "She was all over me."

"Mom." I sound like a kid.

She's head down, listening.

"Okay. I was all over Mr. Rossi. I really was. And he *wouldn't.* He said I was a child—a child to him *now.*"

"That's what this is," Danny says. "She's protecting this guy."

"No," I say. "It's not about that. Mr. Rossi doesn't like me anymore."

Danny's eyes play over me. "That's 'cause he got caught."

Mom looks up.

"So—" I say, "no one would like me unless they were messing with me?"

Danny puts a hand on Mom's chair.

"Mr. Rossi didn't mess with me."

"All right, Angelyn," Mom says.

"*He* stopped liking me."

I'm pointing at Danny.

"Careful, now," he says.

Mom turns to him. "Careful?"

Danny's watching me. "She's geared up for something."

"When he—" I stop. "When Danny—"

"Just a minute." He's rising.

I'm standing too. "You stopped liking me when you got caught."

"*I didn't get caught!* It was that kid," Danny says, "that dopey kid."

"He wasn't so *dopey*. Not about you."

"I've heard enough." Mom speaks evenly.

"Danny touched me." I sag with it.

"You lie!" He shouts it.

I sit, arms curved around my stomach.

"Then you sit too, Dan," Mom says, and I hear him sit, heavily.

"It's a lie," he says.

I raise my eyes. "I'm not lying anymore."

Mom looks back at me.

Danny slouches. "Shut up. Grow up."

"It's hard to grow up," I say. "When my boyfriend touches me, I feel you."

"Boyfriend?" Mom says.

Then there's nothing. For I don't know how long.

"The girl never liked me," Danny says.

"I *loved* you." I search him again. "Did you ever—like me?"

His mouth works like he's chewing tobacco. "No. I never did."

"That's a lie." My voice cracks.

"Angelyn, you leave us to talk," Mom says.

"He's lying. *He* is."

"Go."

I tip the chair, leaving.

I hear Mom ask, "Has it started again?"

■ ■ ■

Has it started again?

It's what I think when I wake up.

How could she ask that?

I check the clock. It's 8:15. Long past our time to leave for her work and my school.

Did she leave me here with him?

Mom is in the kitchen at the window.

"Why didn't you wake me?" I ask.

She leans against the sink. "Have something to eat."

The table holds one set of dishes, used.

"Those are mine," Mom says.

"Where are his?" I ask.

"Danny went out on the job early."

My stomach rumbles. I take an orange. I work on the peel, facing her.

"Mom, what's going to happen?"

She turns. "We're getting your backpack today."

Sacramento is a two-hour run.

"You won't get in trouble on your job, doing this?" I ask as we start.

"Let me worry about my job," Mom says.

"You keep saying you want me to worry about it too."

"Angelyn." Her voice is strained. "I need a day to think. *Away* from here. Is that all right with you?"

Away. "Yes," I say, sitting back.

Morning light floods the truck. We could be twins in ball caps and sunglasses.

I flip the visor down. Mom gets coffee for the drive. I sip Diet Coke. An hour later we stop to pee.

In Manteca we pick up Interstate 5 for the freeway part of the drive. The signs start for Sacramento.

"Do you ever wish we'd stayed?" I ask.

Mom jerks. "Stayed in Sacramento? No. Getting out is what saved us."

"Oh." I was five when we left.

"You don't know what it means to me, coming back and having something now. A job. Some kind of life."

What kind? I think.

"There's plenty you don't know."

I look at Mom. "I didn't say anything."

"No one wanted us here. My family didn't want us."

"They didn't?" I say.

"Danny's the only one who ever gave me more. And I had to leave to find him."

"Do you—*love*—him?" I ask, my mouth twisting. "After last night?"

Mom takes a long breath. "Don't push me."

"I heard you ask if it was happening again. It isn't. What did Danny say?"

"He said no. He said nothing ever did."

I watch her. "The way you asked him, you know that's a lie."

"We're staying in Sacramento tonight," Mom says.

"We are? Why?"

"I'm not only asking him. I've got questions for you."

I laugh.

Mom jabs a finger at me. *"Don't laugh."*

I'm leaning to the window. "It's just— Mom, I said it all last night. If you didn't hear me then, you never will. Or—is all of this *my fault?* 'Cause that's *how I am?*"

"I want to know," she says, "how bad it got."

"Oh."

I look out the side. Rice fields. The endless flats. I remember.

"You want to know—is it worth doing anything about."

"What do you want me to do, Angelyn?" Mom's voice is sharp and sour.

I don't know, I think, and say it.

CHAPTER TWENTY-SIX

Curled on her side, Mom watches me from bed. Cross-legged on mine, I work a comb through shower-wet hair.

"If you'd screamed it," she says, "I would have heard."

I point to the TV. A PBS pledge break. "I'm watching this."

Mom grabs the remote from the nightstand and pops the set off.

The room is dark.

"Not like this," I say.

I hear rustling. A switch flicks. She's got the light on.

"Thanks." Cold in T-shirt and sweats, I climb under the covers.

Mom sits at the edge of her bed. "You never told me anything."

It's hard to look at her. "You never asked."

"You've had three years to say it, Angelyn."

"There never was a time. It was all about Nathan lying and Mrs. Daly being a busybody bitch. You called her that. Remember?"

"Oh, *her*. Miss High and Mighty. She knew better how to raise you."

"We all pretended like nothing was wrong. We've *been* pretending. There was no other way to be. Was there?"

"All right," Mom says. "If I'd asked then, what would you have said?"

I pull my knees up. "Whatever Danny wanted."

"Whatever Danny wanted." She's quiet. "Why?"

"He was my friend. You could be scary." *You are scary.*

"How many times—"

"All you have to know is, it happened."

"I *said*, how many times?"

"Okay." I turn my hands on the smooth sheets. "A baseball season's worth. Part of spring, all summer, part of fall. Is that enough times?"

Mom makes a sound.

I look over. "Every Sunday morning."

"I slept late on Sundays!"

Like she's accusing me.

Deliberately, I say, "Danny would shush me so we wouldn't wake you."

Mom's stare is awful.

"We'd watch TV," I say, "and—"

"I don't want to know," she says.

I push the covers back. "I'm getting some water."

"Get some for me."

I feel better, turned from her, rummaging in the ice bucket. But in the mirror I see Mom staring.

I hand her a tumbler and take mine across the room, to the window. My backpack fills the orange vinyl chair. Next to it, I drain my glass.

"Nathan saw us," I say. "He really did. Ask him. He wasn't lying."

"There's something else you kept quiet." She's drunk her water too. "You've been in touch with that boy. For how long?"

"I sent him off a million times. Nathan hung on. He only just gave up on me."

Mom sits against the pillows. "You've changed. We put this behind us."

"No," I say. "No, we didn't. I think about it all the time."

"You think about Danny?"

I sit on the window ledge. "I think about things being wrong. The lie that happens every day."

Mom *hmm*s. "He said something about you last night."

Despite myself, I ask what.

"Danny said—" She looks at the ceiling. "The two of you used to play like puppies, and maybe his hand slipped once, and maybe you misinterpreted—"

"Twenty-six Sundays, Mom." I say it coldly. "I counted."

"Twenty-six?" Her voice is faint. "I don't believe it. You could have told me. You should have told me."

I let my foot bounce off the wall. "Why? You don't believe it now. And, you know—Danny could have told on himself, back then, if we were *playing like puppies* and his hand slipped. He could have told me—*Sorry.* He could have told you—*I got too close with Angelyn.*"

Mom is quiet.

"Mr. Rossi called me a cat," I say. "Because of how I wrapped up against him. He didn't use it to work me. He told me—" I stop. "He told me, *Go away.*"

Mom stands and walks to the mirror. "You look like me. I've always heard that."

Dark hair, dark eyes. Tall. Long-legged.

"I guess I do."

She slumps onto the bed. "How did we get here?"

"How?" I stand. "You put it all on me. Every bad thing. What do you want me to say, Mom?"

"I didn't know about any of this," she says.

"You acted like you did. You'd tell anyone there's something wrong with me. You said it to Miss Bass and Mr. Rossi—" I'm mad again, remembering. "Mr. Rossi was saying something true about me—right?—and you didn't like it."

Mom raises her head. "I was trying to protect you."

"What?"

"Our—" Mom waves. "Our situation. I was trying to protect that. How do you think it makes *me* look if this is going on and I'm letting it? I work there, Angelyn. I have to keep working there."

I sit. "I go to school there."

She pushes her hair back. "You've got a million chances. I've only got the one."

"But—" I think about that. "I'm your daughter, Mom. You've only got the one."

"Come here," she says after silence.

"Why?" I ask, but I do, sitting across from her.

"How serious are you, Angelyn, about all this?"

I look at Mom. "Serious?"

"It won't be easy," she says. "It will be ugly."

I know what I want. "I want him out."

Mom reaches for the phone.

"I don't want to talk to him," I say, pulling back.

She pushes numbers. They build to ours.

Danny picks up first ring.

"Sherry?" He's breathless.

Mom says, "Be gone when we get back."

CHAPTER TWENTY-SEVEN

Before sunrise I'm at the window, watching traffic.

Mom stirs. "Did you sleep?"

"Not much," I say, shy with her.

She checks the time. "We need to start back."

"Now? It's too early." And: "I don't want to see him."

Mom is up and stretching. "You'll be at school. I'll be at work. Danny has the whole damn day to leave."

I sit against the ledge. "It was real last night. You were serious."

"You bet I was." She's fierce.

"Mom." I can't think what else to say.

She's on her way to the bathroom. "Angelyn, we are moving on."

Mom calls me. Soft, then louder.

I blink awake. "We're here?"

"Almost," she says. "Listen about today."

I uncurl, feeling fuzzy. We're in town, passing Courthouse Park.

"After school you're going to walk to the bus yard and wait with me."

I tell her okay.

"I'll make sure that Danny's gone."

"Just like that," I say.

"Don't doubt it," Mom says.

"You're making it sound easy. You said it would be hard."

"Getting him out is not hard. It's what comes *after* that will be."

"What's that?" I ask, watching her.

"We're reporting him," Mom says.

I sit up. "To the police?"

"Yes. We'll go this afternoon. After school."

"Mom—it's enough for me if Danny isn't around."

"It's not enough for me. He did wrong. He's going to pay."

I sputter. "That means *I* pay. I'd have to get in there—"

She's nodding. "Yes, you'll be involved. Of course you'll be involved."

"I don't want to talk to the cops!"

"Angelyn, you are done protecting him."

My stomach twists. "It wasn't only me who protected him."

"What's that?" Mom says. A real warning.

"Why this, why now?" I ask. Quietly.

"You just be ready," she says. "This afternoon. The sooner we start, the sooner we'll be done."

I turn my head.

"Do you hear me?"

I nod, once.

Then: "Have you forgotten," I say, "that three years ago we told these same police that nothing happened between Danny and me? That nothing ever *could* happen? They will laugh at me—or worse."

Mom says, "I didn't know then. I do now. I'm on it."

My mouth puckers.

"Angelyn, you stop right there."

"Mom, I didn't say anything. But, yeah, I'll shut up. I'm good at that."

"Next we'll work on that attitude." She's icy.

I tug at my seat belt. "You can let me off ahead."

Everyone is in place at Ag. Mom pulls smoothly to the side.

"Which one is your boyfriend? I haven't forgotten that."

"No one," I say, wrestling the backpack out of the cab.

"It's the tall boy, isn't it? The one who's always watching."

I swing around carefully. She means Steve.

"He's just a guy."

"You never told me about him," Mom says.

I pop the door. "Okay. Bye."

"Introduce me to your boyfriend."

I look around. "Mom, no."

"Oh yes," she says. "If he's in your life, then I am going to know him."

I stumble from the truck, dragging the pack, hoping she'll stay inside.

A door opens behind me.

"Mom," I say, clenched teeth, keeping on along the roadside.

She passes me, striding.

"I'm Angelyn's mother," Mom says, stopping at Steve on the sidewalk.

His expression doesn't change. His *no-expression.*

She sticks her hand at him. "I'm Sherry Stark."

His eyes flick from her to me.

"Hey," he says. No color to it.

Her hand floats in the air between them.

Behind Steve, Charity grins. The other kids watch too.

My face is hot. I stand there with the backpack.

Mom stomps past on her way back. Seconds later the truck goes by.

Steve steps off the sidewalk.

"You don't like my mom," I say, walking up.

He shrugs.

"Wait, are you pissed at me too?"

"I'm not thrilled," Steve says.

I lean away from him. "Why?"

"You never came back on Monday when you went off with that girl."

"Oh." Monday is forever ago. "Well, lunch was almost over."

Steve says, "Okay, and what about yesterday?"

I look at him blankly.

"The reservoir, Angelyn. You said you'd go. I waited for you—again."

The reservoir. "I was out of town. Mom took me to Sacramento."

He dips his chin. "Bet that broke your heart."

Charity laughs.

I focus on Steve. "I had a shit time. Does that make it better?"

"Nope. You have got to stop flaking on me."

It's one thing too many. My eyes fill. I can't help it.

I shoulder the pack. "See you."

He catches a strap. "Wait."

We face each other.

Steve points to the backpack. "Your mom took you for that, right?"

I nod. "Got the backpack. Yay."

He squints. "What else happened?"

"What do you mean?"

"To make it a shit time."

Damn.

"Angelyn, hey."

I wipe my eyes. "Don't ask me that."

"I'm asking. This whole thing is too weird, and me not knowing."

"*Weird* is a good word for it," I say.

"Tell me what's going on and maybe we can get somewhere."

"Where do you want us to be?" I ask.

"I want us to be like we were," Steve says slowly.

I shake my head. "No."

He takes a step in. "Ange." Charity adjusts, peeking around.

I flip a hand at her, and the rest. *"They're* always here. Can't they all go someplace else?"

Steve looks. "Oh, them. *Shoo.*" He waves his arms. *"Git!"*

Most of the kids pretend to be doing something else. Charity pouts.

I fight a smile. "I can still see them."

He walks in tight. "How about now?"

I see his chest, his collarbone, his shoulders. Him.

"Steve. This is not what I want."

He stuffs his hands in his pockets. "This is me blocking your view. That's all I'm doing."

I look up. "Why can't you be an ass *all* the time? So I'd know."

A flicker of a grin. "Angelyn, stay. Anything else, we'll figure it out."

I blink at him. "Mostly, I'm tired. I only want to rest."

Steve says, "Rest here." Very quiet. "I miss you when you're not around."

I stand with him outside their eyes.

"You missed yesterday," Mr. Rossi says when I come into World Cultures.

I barely look at him. "I'll get a note."

The girls are at their desks. They stop talking as I come down the aisle.

Jacey lowers her eyes. Charity watches with bright curiosity.

"Hi," I say deliberately.

Charity purses her lips. "Angelyn, are you *okay*?"

I slam in—"Just great!"—and drop my backpack at my feet.

"That was *so sad*," she says, "outside, when you were crying."

"I was not crying." *Shut up, Angelyn! Shut up.*

Charity's desk creaks. "Steve told us you were never coming back."

It takes the breath out of me, him talking.

Jacey looks over. "That was all he said, Angelyn."

I nod to her, stiffly.

The bell rings. Mr. Rossi stands and calls for the homework.

I unzip the backpack and dig out my text. Thumbing through, I find last week's homework. Thursday's work. I don't have Friday's work, or Monday's, or yesterday's. Three zeroes. No, four. Mr. Rossi doesn't take late work.

I suck.

No one is passing work forward. People are switching seats.

I look at Jacey. "What's going on?"

She picks at her book cover. "That report thing."

Shit. "The report's due now?"

"Part of it, I think. He said yesterday."

"Angelyn!" Charity says. "Did you get the notes from that girl?"

Jeni's notes. I remember getting them. "Yeah," I say shortly.

The noise around us rises. Even the back-row boys look busy.

Mr. Rossi says my name.

"What?" I say, not too friendly.

"Your partner isn't here."

"No," I say. "She won't be."

"That makes you group leader. And spokesman for your project."

I shrug, feeling slightly sick.

"You up for it?" he asks.

"Oh, always," I say. The girls snicker.

His face pinks. "Moving on. Dylan, start us off. Your group had India."

The Dylan kid stands, rattling off statistics like he's been programmed. I dip into my backpack, pushing books aside, flipping through papers, searching for Jeni's small and neat printing.

Charity's desk scrapes mine. "You're going to use the notes, aren't you?"

I slide forward. "Don't talk to me."

Dylan finishes. Mr. Rossi marks something on a clipboard.

"Who's next?" He scans the class. "Angelyn. Are you ready?"

"I was absent."

"Yes, but you've had time to come up with something."

"Jeni did. I mean, *we* did, together, but—"

"What I need to know is where you're at."

"Jeni's gone." My voice rasps.

"So, what do *you* have?" Mr. Rossi says.

Charity whispers, "Use the notes!"

I grip my backpack. "Can you come back to me?"

"Sure. Katie James. Tell us about your project."

Katie—one of three Katies in the room—stands.

"Our group has China. We're doing the Cultural Revolution. Its history, background, impact, and aftermath."

She goes on. How they've divided the tasks. The research they've done. The docu-short they're producing for the class.

I hunch over the pack, pulling stuff out, piling it on my desk. On the bottom, my notebook, curved from the weight of everything else. Not Jeni's notes.

A glance at Katie, I flip pages. Most are blank. On one, the heading:

AUSTRALIA

Under it, the notes I took:

English prisons; convicts; transport ships; work it off.

And:

Start over!!

I stare at the words. I remember writing them. I remember talking with Jeni.

Charity hisses something.

Katie finishes.

Mr. Rossi walks to our row. "Ms. Flint. What have you and Ms. Jordan been working on?"

Charity doesn't answer.

"You girls had Italy. Where did your research take you?"

"We're in Angelyn's group now," she says.

I look around. "What?"

Charity winks. "Remember how we talked about switching?"

Jacey checks us both.

"That girl left," Charity says. "Everyone knows that we three work together."

Mr. Rossi says, "I don't know it. Angelyn?"

"I'm not with them," I say.

Charity says, "Yes, you are! You're back with Steve."

I flinch. "Don't talk about me."

"What happens outside class does not concern me," Mr. Rossi says.

"She wants Jeni's notes," I say.

"Do not!" Charity says.

I stare at her. "And I don't have them. I don't even have them."

She sits back. "Angelyn, you lie."

My gut swirls. "Come up and search me."

"All right," Mr. Rossi says. "Nobody's switching groups."

I face front, an arm around my notebook.

"Charity. Jacey. Do you have work to share?"

The only sound is the scratching of his pen.

Mr. Rossi looks up. "Angelyn, what do you have?"

I swallow. "Not much."

"Something, though."

"Yes," I say.

He sits against his desk. "Let's hear it."

"Our country was Australia." My voice is thin. Hoarse.

"Stand, please."

I drag myself up.

"Australia's made up of lots of different kinds of people. Sort of like the U.S."

Chin on hand, Mr. Rossi listens.

"There were the people who were already there."

"Indigenous peoples," he says.

"And the ones who came later, from outside."

"So smart," Charity says.

He points at her. "Stop." And waves me on.

"Some of the first who came—they were sent. Convicts. Australia was supposed to be their punishment."

"Who sent them?" Mr. Rossi asks.

"England," I say. "English courts. It didn't take much to be in trouble then. People were really poor and stealing food and getting hanged for it. Kids, even. So, they started sending them to Australia instead."

Mr. Rossi nods. "All right. What's your angle?"

"My angle? What happened to them, I guess. The convicts."

"You need more. How did this affect Australia as a nation?"

I glance at my notes. "That must have been Jeni's part."

"Come on, Angelyn. Think."

"Whatever they did," I say, "whyever they were sent, in Australia they could work it off. Make it good. Instead of sitting in some English prison or dying for it."

Mr. Rossi circles a hand. "And?"

I remember something. "They couldn't go back."

"No?"

"They weren't supposed to. Even after they'd worked off their time. That was hard for some, because, you know, England was the mother country. Jeni showed me this article that said people were still ashamed—" I stumble on the word. "Years later."

"Keep going," Mr. Rossi says.

"Convicts and their kids and even grandkids," I say. "*Ashamed* and looking back to England. This article said, don't look back. Because what they built *there* is better than anything that could have come before."

I let the chair take my weight. Done.

Mr. Rossi stands. "That was good."

I study my hands. "Uh-huh."

"No. It was. Tie what you said into the Australian identity and—yeah."

I look at him. "Really?"

He smiles. "Really."

Pride shoots through me. "Okay." I try to sound cool.

Mr. Rossi looks off. "Eric. Tell us about Vietnam."

Eric grabs up note cards. "Sure, give me a minute."

"That wasn't Angelyn's work," Charity says.

My body tenses.

Mr. Rossi is marking something on the clipboard.

"Hello?" Charity says. "Mr. Rossi?"

He frowns. "Yes, Ms. Flint?"

"Angelyn got those notes from that girl. The ideas. Everything."

My hands curl. "Her name is Jeni."

"Angelyn, don't respond," Mr. Rossi says. "Ms. Flint, you let me worry."

"I don't think it's right," Charity says. "Her getting an A."

He sets the board down. "Today is about points. No one gets an A."

"Then why does she get the *points*?"

I face her. "Bitch, I don't have Jeni's notes."

"It isn't *fair*," Charity says past me.

"Shut the fuck up."

Her eyes get wide. "You can't say that!"

Mr. Rossi says my name with force.

"What?" My voice crackles.

"She's right. You can't talk that way in here."

"*She's* right? She isn't right about anything."

He points to the desk by the window. "Move."

Charity says, "Ha!"

"After class I'll speak to you both."

"*Me?*" she says as I stare at the mess on my desk.

"No," I say.

Up the aisle, people are talking. All I can see is the door.

Mr. Rossi steps in front. "Where are you going?"

"Out," I say, stopped between desks.

"I can excuse you for a few minutes, but—"

"I don't belong here."

His face softens. "Sure you do. Of course you do. More than some."

"Oh—you're being *nice* again."

"Take a seat. We'll talk after class."

"You said we couldn't talk."

Mr. Rossi clears his throat. "Angelyn."

I press ahead. "I'm going."

He stands firm at the head of the aisle. I try to wind around. Mr. Rossi blocks me again.

"I don't want you to leave like this," he says.

"Let me by," I say, not looking at him.

Mr. Rossi says no.

A moment, and I charge. Falling back, he grabs my arms. I wrench free.

"Freakin' perv, let me go!"

I stop in the doorway, facing the hall.

Behind me, Mr. Rossi says, "Don't go." His voice is unsteady.

"Why not?" My voice shakes too.

"You did a good thing here. Don't waste it."

"I already screwed things up. I screwed them up with you."

"Don't make it worse," Mr. Rossi says.

I turn. "You told on me. *You* told Miss Bass. Didn't you?"

"Yes." He glances back. "Now is not the time to discuss it."

I see the class behind him. Caught up in every word.

"You don't know me." I say it anyway. "You *play* me. Hot and cold. You lift me up. Set me down. When do I know to believe you?"

Mr. Rossi is pale. "I meant every good thing."

That stops me. "You did?" My voice is soft, like a kid's. I frown after.

"Angelyn," he says. "You're crossing some lines here. They're lines that you don't need to cross."

"I'm sorry." I say it automatically. Then, again: "I'm sorry."

"Come in," Mr. Rossi says. "We'll talk after class. I promise."

"You promised before." But I step back in. I can't meet his eyes or anyone's.

"Good." He makes way for me. "Now, let's finish the period."

I start across the room for the desk by the window.

I hear them:

"Freakin' perv! Tight."

"Why'd she call him that?"

"She's crazy."

"What about him?"

"'Hot 'n' cold.' Oww."

"Angelyn always did like older guys." Charity.

I stop. "Huh?"

Her expression: *Gotcha.* I check Jacey. Who's scarlet.

My throat closes. "You—said something?"

Jacey says, *"No."* Her head wags long after the word.

"We talk about you," Charity says. *"All the time.* And I *know."*

I'm stuck, facing the girls and the class. Some kids are grinning. Others whisper. Jacey's head bends to her desk.

"You're not so special," Charity says.

Her face balloons to a target. *The* target. And it's all of it. All of it.

I charge the aisle. Mr. Rossi shouts after me.

I make a fist and aim it.

CHAPTER TWENTY-EIGHT

Kicked out.

"Kicked *out*?"

Mom is pacing.

"What'll I do with you now, Angelyn?"

From my inch of couch, I study the empty table that once held our TV.

"Is he coming back for more?" I ask.

She stops. "Danny would have carried that couch out on his back if he could."

"I wish he had," I say, standing.

Our eyes meet. Same height.

"Is Danny coming back?"

"Danny's running scared," Mom says.

His truck was gone when we pulled in. His clothes. Personal things. The TV.

"Meanwhile—" Mom says.

I look away. "What happened at school had to happen."

"With *that* girl. In *that* teacher's classroom."

"Yeah."

"You put me in Miss Bass's office again, Angelyn. And she's

looking at me like this is *my* fault. She told me to take tomorrow off to be with you."

I shrug.

"Do you have any idea how much trouble you're in?"

"I know I'm suspended."

"Suspended *plus*," Mom says. "Weren't you even listening?"

"I guess I wasn't."

"The school is working up a behavior contract on you. We have to sign it to get you back in. Once they have that, you cross the line in any direction and you are gone—expelled from Blue Creek."

"Gone," I say. "From Mr. Rossi's class?"

"That's already happened."

I move to the window. "Who made it happen? You or him?"

"You're not hearing me," Mom says.

I pull the curtain back. "You're not hearing me."

"Charity's mother might press charges. Does that get through?"

I touch my forehead to the glass. The house across is empty still.

"Do you want to be in *jail*?" Mom's voice sharpens.

A neighbor dog trots by, barely kept, its nose to the darkened pavement.

"I want to be somewhere else," I say.

"You—what? Well, that's just great. I sent him away for you! This is what I get back?"

I turn. "Do it *BECAUSE IT'S RIGHT*."

Mom breathes in, a hand to her chest. "Go to your room and stay there."

I scrape past. Nothing to say to her, forever.

My bed is shaking.

I slide up against the pillows.

A shape shifts at the end of the bed.

My heart knocks. "Mom, what do you want?"

She's crying. "What did Danny get off you he couldn't get from me?"

"Ask him." Her words connect. "Don't say that to me! You're my mother."

"What did you tell that boyfriend of yours? The way he looked at me."

"I told him nothing." It's easier in the dark. "He's seen the way you treat me. Maybe he thinks it stinks."

"I'm better with you than my mother was with me."

"How would I know that, Mom? You never talk about her. You never talk about anything that came before this town."

"There's nothing to say. My mother had no use for me. She kicked me out when I was seventeen. Seventeen, pregnant, and on my own."

"With me," I say.

"Yes, with you. But what could you do, a baby? I made my way in this world alone."

I want to laugh. I laugh. "You always had a guy around. Different guys, before him. Different people, all the time. I remember."

Mom blows her nose in something. "Everybody needs help sometimes."

You never gave me any. I think it and say it out loud.

"I kept him from you," Mom says.

"What?"

"Danny never touched you after that. I saw to it."

I flip the light on. Her face is blotchy. She's red-eyed. Dressed still in T-shirt and jeans.

"You said I never asked you about him. Angelyn, we couldn't afford the answer. Not then."

The air tastes sour.

"Listen to me," Mom says, though I haven't interrupted. "I couldn't pay the *rent* on this place. Not alone. With him I was able to buy it."

"You knew," I say. "You did know."

Mom swipes at her eyes. "I *suspected*. I didn't know."

I take it in. "Mrs. Daly—the way you treated her. Nathan."

"I kept my family together. That is what we needed."

"Mom. The way you've treated me."

She's quiet. "I've always done the best I could."

"Can you leave me alone now?" I ask. Quiet too.

"Don't be hating me!" Mom says. "I always meant to knock him out of our lives. I would have too. You just couldn't wait."

"I guess I was having too much fun, the way things were."

She stands. Paces. I draw in tight, arms around elbows.

"We'll go to the police in the morning," Mom says. "Bright and early."

"Why bother?"

"I'm a mandated reporter. I will be, once I'm licensed and certified as a school bus driver. Do you know what that means? I have to report any abuse situation. I *have* to. It's the law."

I look up at her. "I'm your daughter, not some random kid on your bus."

"The point is," Mom says, "now I know how to do this. Now I *can* do it."

I don't know what I feel.

"Now that it's out—now that you're talking about this, Angelyn—I'm going to support you. We'll do things the right way."

I'm thinking through three years of *stuff.*

"Say something." Mom is staring.

"In Mr. Rossi's class," I say, "I did this report. He liked it. Charity stomped on it, and then she said she knew about Danny and me. That's why I punched her."

Mom pulls out my desk chair and sits. "How would that girl know?"

"I told another friend back when it was happening. Jacey. She must have told Charity."

"But that's good! Jacey could come with us and tell the police."

"No, Mom. Those girls don't really like me. They think I'm trash. And—they think you are."

"I know what people think. I don't let it stop me. You shouldn't either."

"I'm not asking Jacey. No way."

"You know," Mom says, "it wasn't Mr. Rossi or me who pulled you from that class. Charity's mother asked for that. She didn't want her little darling competing."

His hands, pulling me off Charity. His voice, hard. What he said:

"Let's go."

Something else:

"She isn't worth it."

"Is Mr. Rossi all right?"

Mom sits back. "Is he all right? Worry about *this*, Angelyn. Worry about *us*."

"I might have got him in trouble." I shake my head at her expression. "I called him something bad. I said it in front of everyone."

"What?" she says.

"Something he didn't deserve."

Mom studies me. "What happened—for real—between you and Mr. Rossi?"

"Nothing. For real. Mr. Rossi didn't go there."

Our eyes hold. I look away.

"Is that what he taught you?" Mom asks.

"Yeah." My voice is thick.

"I heard he's taking some time off."

I sit up, icy-shower awake. "Mr. Rossi is? Why?"

"I don't know. It's not my concern. Or yours."

I twist in bed, wanting to do—something. Say something, to someone who'll hear.

Mom checks the clock. "I've got to try to sleep. We both have to be fresh for the morning."

She turns at the door. "So, you see—I would have thrown Danny out if I could. I would have asked you about him *if I could*. Angel, I couldn't. You get that, don't you?"

"Angel," I say. "You called me that when I was little."

"Yes," Mom says. With a smile. "Things will be better here without him. You'll see."

Sick, frozen smile.

I clear my throat. "Do you really think I have a million chances, Mom?"

She nods. "You can make something of yourself. Like I did."

"I will leave to do that," I say. "Like you did."

Mom's smile deflates. "You're finishing high school, Angelyn."

"I'll finish. I'm gone after that."

She straightens, a hand to the doorframe. "You hold to that. You make your own life."

I look at her steadily. "I will."

"Nine a.m.," Mom says, her face in profile. "We're going to the cops."

Next Morning

At eight a.m. she's still asleep. I'm on the landing outside the kitchen, on the phone to Steve.

■ ■ ■

He squints at me. "I wish you'd say where we're going."

"You said you'd do this," I remind him.

Steve grunts.

"And you wouldn't ask questions."

We pass the elementary school where I went. Nathan went. Not Steve. I didn't know him then.

"Thanks for doing this," I say.

He nods. "Jacey was there when you called. She said to tell you hey."

"Tell her—tell her *nothing*."

Steve looks over. "Charity's out, you know."

"Good," I say.

He chuckles.

I don't smile. "I'm done with them."

We start onto the country road. I flip the visor. A bright fall day, the light more white than gold.

"I was thinking," Steve says. "We could try something new."

"Like what?" I ask.

"We could go out like other people do."

I check him. "What other people?"

"*Most* other people. I'd take you to the movies, bowling, whatever. It wouldn't just be seeing each other at school."

The old hurt flares. "You didn't want any of that the time I asked."

Steve says, "You mean when I was at your house for the first time ever, and we'd been together a year?"

I lift a shoulder. "There were reasons for that."

"I had my reasons too, that night. I didn't know what you were after."

"You only knew what *you* wanted," I say.

"Angelyn, let's don't fight. It's good you called me. That's a start."

"I needed a ride." Steve winces. "I didn't know anyone else who'd drive me. I thought, maybe, you'd want to do a friend a favor."

"I did," he says. "I do."

"Steve, all you cared about before was getting in me. What changed?"

"I keep trying to tell you. I didn't know—I couldn't do without you."

"Oh," I say.

"We could find a way to be together," he says. "We could find a way for both of us."

"There would always be them," I say. "Your friends."

"Forget them! I'm talking about us."

I turn to the window. "Everything's together. You know it is."

"I'd stand up for you, Angelyn. I swear I would. Things would be *different*. We'd make them different."

In quiet I watch the passing scene, remembering that first trip with Mr. Rossi. The second one with Nathan where I couldn't see a thing.

"You can't forget I left that dog," Steve says with lowered voice.

The trees are thinning, the houses coming through.

"Hell, my dad told me to shoot it. I didn't. I couldn't."

"I'm glad you didn't." I sound a million miles off.

"You want to be alone," Steve says. "Alone without anyone. You really do."

I nod. "I want to try things on my own."

"I want to be with you, Angelyn. Yeah. And know you. Wouldn't you want me—if things were like that?"

"No, Steve." I look at him. "Too much happened."

"Too much, huh?" His voice is strained.

"I don't mean to hurt you."

"Hey, I'm all right," he says.

I turn back to the window. "Around the next corner, I think."

I tell Steve to park on the roadside. He pulls in past the driveway, under a cluster of oaks.

"I won't be long," I say.

"Okay."

Outside I stand in a tangle of weeds, a hand on the side of the truck.

Steve switches the radio on. Country music.

I walk around. "Hey."

He looks at me, no expression.

"Are you going to wait for me?" I ask. "I get it if you don't want to. I can walk back. But I want to know if you're going to be here or not."

"I'm waiting for you, Angelyn," Steve says. "Friends don't leave."

CHAPTER TWENTY-NINE

The driveway is rutted. Not easy to walk. I stay to the side like I did in the dark, scuffing browned oleander petals and slippery oak leaves. Gravel crackles underneath, noisy to me like popping bubble wrap. I listen for Dolly, expecting her. I only hear myself.

Around the turn to Mr. Rossi's place, I stop, look, and listen hard. His car is in the detached garage. Dolly's leash is on the lead, but she's not on it. The house is closed and quiet.

"Dolly?" I say. Scared, a little.

Faintly, I hear a sound like *clip clip*. Metal on metal.

The pool is covered, a slick blue vinyl throwing back sun. I shade my eyes, passing. He's buzzed the lawn.

I call her: "Dolly!"

In the distance, an answering bark. I smile.

She comes running from behind the house, fur combed to feathery swirls along her belly.

My smile stretches. "Hey there!"

Dolly circles, wagging her body. I fold into the spiky grass, arms out. She climbs in and licks my chin. I hold her close. So warm and good.

"Angelyn?"

Mr. Rossi stands above. Sweaty, bits of brush stuck to his T-shirt and jeans.

"I was working out back," he says. Then: "Why are you here?"

"Please," I say. "Please don't be mad."

"You shouldn't be here," Mr. Rossi says.

"I know."

"It isn't good for you or me that you're here."

I look at Dolly, curled in my lap. "You didn't do anything wrong."

"Now I'll have to ask you to leave," he says.

I touch her silky ear. "I wanted to see if you were all right. Are you, Mr. Rossi?"

"Am I—?" He's quiet. "Sure I am. How about you?"

"Oh. Suspended," I say. "And other things."

"We can't be having this conversation."

I raise my eyes. "Are you in trouble over me?"

Mr. Rossi says no.

"But—we're both out of school today. Like you're suspended too."

"I said I'm all right."

"I'm sorry for what happened in class."

Mr. Rossi nods. "You know you have to go."

I pet Dolly. "Maybe I could take her."

"What? Take the dog?"

"You don't want her. And, well, I do."

Dolly licks my arm.

I see us at the frosty. Dolly, Steve, and me. I'm sharing my hamburger, and he's flicking fries. Dolly snaps them from the air. We're laughing.

"How did you get here?" Mr. Rossi asks.

"Steve brought me. He's out there."

"Steve brought you. Coslow."

"We're not together," I say. "Friends, sort of."

Mr. Rossi rubs his neck. "So, if you walk out with this dog he dumped weeks ago—that'll be okay?"

"Why not? She'd be mine."

"It's all right, then, with your folks? They told you, *Get a dog*?"

"My stepdad moved out. My mom? She owes me."

"That's where you want to bring Dolly? To a place your mom 'owes' you?"

I lean over her. "Dolly would be *mine*. Not my mom's or anyone else's."

Mr. Rossi says, "She's found her place here."

Face hidden, I frown.

"What's best for the animal? Ask yourself that."

"Mr. Rossi, I'd treat her like gold! Don't you know I would?"

"I know that you'd want to." He crouches. "I'm not being fair. I want the dog."

"*You* do?"

He nods to the porch. "Come on. We can talk."

I sit with him on the steps, sipping lemonade he's brought out. Dolly stretched on the cool concrete below.

"She's worked out great," Mr. Rossi says. "She's a good fit. My son likes her."

"Your son?"

"Camden was here this weekend." He says it like sunlight.

"Oh." I stare at my feet, lined up with his.

"Things are different for me now. Better."

"You mean with you and your wife?"

"With everything," Mr. Rossi says.

"How can they be," I ask, "after what happened at school?"

"The school is not my life."

"But—they made you take time off."

"The time off was my decision."

"Mr. Rossi, you don't have to protect me. I called you— *that*—in front of everyone. I want to make it right. I'll talk to any of them—Miss Bass, the principal. I want to tell the truth about you."

He sets his glass down. "Angelyn, I don't need you to do that. I'm a big boy."

"But not a *freakin' perv*. You never were."

Our eyes catch.

"Someone in your life was," Mr. Rossi says.

"Yes," I say.

"I wondered. I'm sorry."

"It's all right. He's gone now."

Mr. Rossi looks off. "I am sorry. I might have helped you."

"You did help me. You so did."

"If that's true, I'm glad."

"It's what you *didn't* do, Mr. Rossi."

"I crossed some lines," he says. "Things got rough here for a while."

"Lines," I say. "Like, saving Dolly? Letting me stay over? Taking me to see Mrs. Daly?"

"I got to be more than a teacher to you," he says. "I saw you as more than a student."

"Is that bad?" I ask. "Is it always bad? You weren't like him. You never used me."

Mr. Rossi sighs. "I'm taking the time to figure some things out. About teaching, about me, and my family."

"Okay," I say because I can't think what else.

He shifts around, his back to the rail. "You know, you weren't wrong in the classroom."

I stretch my legs. "But I shouldn't have hit her."

Dolly lifts her head, watching.

"Right," Mr. Rossi says. "You put the outcome in her hands."

"I have to sign some stuff before they'll let me back. They're going to be watching me. Everyone is."

"Probably," he says. "Work through it. You've got a brain, Angelyn. A good mind."

"I'll work through it. I know I'll never have another teacher like you."

"Be a student," Mr. Rossi says. "You'll be surprised what can happen when you go in thinking like that."

I nod, hoping he's right.

Mr. Rossi dusts his knees. "Well—"

I'm not ready for the end. "You and your wife are okay now?"

His face clouds. "For Camden's sake, we're working on it."

"Will you tell me, Mr. Rossi? Why was she so pissed?"

He looks at me. "I spent time with someone I shouldn't have."

I catch my breath.

"No, not you. And, no, I won't say who."

Mr. Rossi stands. I stand after him.

"I shouldn't have asked."

"No," he says. "You shouldn't have."

We face each other on the ground.

"It's cool your son likes Dolly." I lean for a pet. "But, you know, I love her."

"I know you do," Mr. Rossi says. "Can you love her enough to let her go?"

Tears push at me. I bite my cheek.

"Angelyn, I want to ask you something."

"What?"

"Do you know Ms. Jones in the Career Center?"

"I know who she is," I say.

"She knows about you," Mr. Rossi says. "How you're interested in the Coast Guard."

"I'm not. Anymore."

"You're sure about that?"

I fold my arms. "I wanted to talk about it with you."

"That's not going to happen." Mr. Rossi is gentle.

"How does Ms. Jones know about me?"

"I told her," he says. "I gave her my student's email—the one who joined the Coast Guard. It's all set for you to contact her. If you want."

"How would I have known if I didn't come here?"

"I told Ms. Jones to keep an eye out," Mr. Rossi says.

"For me?"

"Yes," he says. "For you."

"Oh." My head drops.

"What's this?"

I press my eyes with cold fingers. "Me being happy."

"Angelyn?"

"It's dumb. You care."

Mr. Rossi says, "That's not so hard to do."

I fix on Dolly. "That night I stayed here. You held me. You were drunk and I needed to be held. I was so happy. Did you know you were doing it?"

He doesn't answer.

"That's all you did, Mr. Rossi. Hold me. And I held you. Do you remember?"

Still quiet.

I point over my shoulder. "I guess I better go."

"Be well," he says. Dolly sits beside him, ears cocked.

"I think you were right," I say. "She's better here."

"I'm glad," Mr. Rossi says. "You know this has to be the last time you come by."

I toss my hair. "I know. You don't have to tell me."

"Okay."

Nothing left to say. For either of us.

"Well—bye."

"Goodbye, Angelyn."

I'm shaky, moving off. One foot in front of the other. I have to think it. Something left unsaid. Undone.

I walk back. Mr. Rossi watches, his face still.

"Thank you for being my fr—*teacher*," I say. "Thank you for being my teacher and friend."

He smiles. "You bet."

A moment we're there, standing close.

"See you, Mr. Rossi."

"See you, Angelyn."

Wind swirls dust out of the gravel as I leave the path. I wave it off, swallowing some. Trying not to cough. I wonder if he's watching. I squint at the pool, remembering the thick chill the night I jumped in. The warmth afterward. Past it, I hear a scrabble of nails. Dolly. My heart lifts.

"Hey!" when she reaches me. I drop to my knees. The rocks dig in.

Dolly wriggles in my arms.

"You want to go with me, huh? You want to be with me."

She licks my hand, holding her in place.

Dolly, my dog.

Stretched on my bed, there every morning.

Living my life.

I press my face to her neck. "You stay here. Home."

I kiss Dolly. I let her go.

She looks at me and back to the house.

"That's right," I say. "Go home."

I wait for him to call her. He doesn't.

"Baby, go home," I say, and I point, and look.

Mr. Rossi is standing. Watching. I raise my hand.

He raises his. And whistles. "Dolly!"

A whisk of her feathery tail against my arm and she is off.

I brush my cheeks and rise and move ahead toward my home.